HARM

BRIAN W. ALDISS

DUCKWORTH OVERLOOK

This edition published in 2008 by
Duckworth Overlook
90-93 Cowcross Street, London, EC1M 6BF
Tel: 020 7490 7300
Fax: 020 7490 0080
info@duckworth-publishers.co.uk
www.ducknet.co.uk

First published in the United States by Del Rey Books,
an imprint of The Random House Publishing Group,
a division of Random House, Inc., New York.

This edition published by arrangement with Ballantine Books, an imprint
of Random House Publishing Group, a division of Random House, Inc.

This is a work of fiction. Names, characters, places and incidents
are the products of the author's imagination or are used fictitiously.
Any resemblance to actual events, locales, or persons,
living or dead, is entirely confidential.

A catalogue record for this book is available from the British Library

ISBN 978 0 7156 3762 3

Book design by Susan Turner
Printed and bound in Great Britain by
Creative Print & Design, Blaina, Wales

This story is dedicated to those who cannot yet read,
my grandsons, Archie and Max,
and to those who now can, Thomas, Laurence, and Jason,
in the hope that they may
all live in a more harmless world than ours.

I am all-powerful Time which destroys all things,
and I have come here to destroy these men.
Even if thou dost not fight,
all the warriors facing thee shall die.

KRISHNA, in the Bhagavad Gita 11:32

And he was afraid, and said,
How dreadful is this place!
This is none other than the house of God.

Genesis 28

In the name of God, the Compassionate, the Merciful
"Unbelievers, I do not worship what you worship,
Nor do you worship what I worship. I shall never worship
what you worship, nor will you ever worship what I
worship. You have your own religion and I have mine."

Koran 109:1

The Master said:
"If one has heard the Way in the morning,
it is all right to die in the evening."

CONFUCIUS, *The Analects*, Book 4

HARM

ONE

Authority ordained it. Lesser authoritarians carried out its orders. No nation ever lacks those who will carry out orders.

The man this tale concerns was taken into custody. There had been a carefree time for foolishness, but that time was gone. This was the time for seriousness, for a war against terror. A nation's security was at stake.

Certain liberties had to be curtailed — such as foolishness and satire and freedom of speech. They belonged to a bygone epoch. Now there was a new epoch. "Every man must brace himself against the hidden enemy among us." So it said in the leaflet.

The captive was hooded and shackled. He was young, although already aged by imprisonment and the fears imprisonment brings. Two soldiers pushed or dragged him along, complaining about the difficulty of the task as they went. They moved down a long corridor. Military boots echoed on tile. A door was opened. The prisoner was flung inside an empty room. A door slammed behind him.

He was known as Prisoner B.

PRISONER B LAY WHERE HE WAS, sprawled on the floor. Slowly he pulled himself into a sitting position and dragged the hood from his head. He simply sat there, breathing shallowly, trying to recover his wits. His ribs ached from the recent beating.

Gradually he became aware of his surroundings. He was in a large room, not a cell. The room was windowless. Such light as there was was supplied by a naked bulb far overhead. He crawled on hands and knees to the nearest wall. It was covered with a floral wallpaper, now faded. Evidently the room had been pressed into use as a cell for prisoners. Evidently, too, this place in which he found himself had once been a grand mansion, a mansion by no means devised for its present ends.

Leaning against the wall for stability, Prisoner B made himself stand. In one corner he saw a bucket and managed to walk over to it, where he relieved himself.

He propped himself against the wall, pressing the palms of his hands against it to stop their trembling. When he attempted to consider his situation, no thought came to him. He was simply a prisoner, totally within the power of his captors.

The hours passed. He had nothing to do but await the next spell of interrogation. It was impossible to imagine anything beyond the walls of this prison.

A bench stood against the far wall. He went over to it. An ordinary garden bench had been brought inside, presumably to serve as a bed. In his weakness, he lay down on it. The bench was too short for any sort of comfort. His legs dangled over the end of it. In any case, he felt too drained to get up.

After a while, he fell into a feverish kind of sleep.

Two guards came and woke Prisoner B in what he believed to be the middle of the night. They wore rough civilian clothes. He was slightly encouraged by this and asked them, as they hauled him into the corridor, "Where am I?"

They gave no answer.

"I mean, what *country* are we in?"

One of the men said, "We're in fucking Syria, aren't we?"

Fresh terror assailed him. "Syria? It can't be. I thought Syria was an enemy state."

"Shut the fuck up" was the only response.

They took him to one of the interrogation rooms.

He was in a small room with what he took to be a Turkish decoration on one wall. A voiceless thing within his head kept repeating "Syria, Syria, Syria." In his disturbed state, he could not recall where Syria was. But there was little chance for anything resembling speculation. Soldiers stood alertly in the room, cuddling carbines. He was made to stand before a desk, behind which sat a thin man with a square jaw and heavy eyebrows. His head was shaven.

He sat quietly, his large red hands folded on the desktop, regarding his prisoner through a pair of unblinking eyes.

"Are you okay?" he asked. A friendly enough opening.

"Fine."

"Then stand up properly. You're not in whatever stinking hole you came from." He paused. "I shall ask you some questions. You will answer without lying. Understand?"

When Prisoner B nodded, the interrogator roared, "Do you bloody well understand?"

He switched on a desk lamp so that the beam shone in Prisoner B's eyes.

"Yes, I understand." He lifted a hand to shade his eyes.

"Put your lousy hand down. What age are you?"

"Twenty-one."

"What age will you be next year at this time?"

"Twenty-two."

"Twenty-two or dead. Say it."

"Twenty-two or dead."

"Name your father."

He did so.

"Name your mother."

He did so.

"Name all your brothers."

He did so.

"Name your sister."

He did so.

"She is a filthy prostitute."

"No."

"She is a filthy stinking prostitute, I said. She is in another room even now, servicing our soldiers of low rank."

"Not by choice."

"Of course by choice. She can't get enough of it. You are here because of a report from ISID incriminating you."

"I don't even know what ISID is."

"Don't play the fucking innocent with me. ISID is the Pakistani antiterrorist organization. What is your job?"

"Writer."

"Why do you write lies?"

"I don't."

"You are paid to write lies about us."

"No."

"You are paid to write lies, you little bastard!"

"No. What lies do you mean?"

"You wrote this filthy book, *Pied Piper of Hament.* There you slandered the religion and the leader."

"No. You cannot prove I did that."

"You did. You were flogged for it."

Silence.

"Why was the book published in countries hostile to us?"

"It won critical approval."

"Do you know these bastards?"

"What bastards?"

The interrogator read from a laudatory section of a foreign review. "It says, 'Some of the scenes in the novel are particularly vivid, particularly those set in London. The Changing of the Guard at Buckingham Palace is most amusing, described as a relic of an old imperial system, now redesigned as a tourist attraction.' And so on . . ."

"That critique contains some inaccuracies. I was never in that reviewer's country."

"Yes, you were. The year before last. We have proof."

"Oh yes, just for two days."

"You stinking treacherous liar."

Prisoner B was kicked from behind, again and again, on his buttocks and thighs.

"That's enough! How long have you been a member of Al-Muhajiroun?"

"I don't even know what it is."

"You bloody liar! It's an extremist Islamic group, full of evil bastards and suicide bombers. A man was arrested last week in Kensal Town, in the street next to yours. You belong to this group."

"I certainly don't. Are you arresting everyone in Kensal Town?"

"Look, don't try to be funny with me, you shit! We're just carrying out EU policy."

They beat him up.

The interrogation lasted for another hour.

Prisoner B had heard most of the questions before.

AS HE WAS BEING DRAGGED BACK TO HIS CELL, a bell rang. His escort halted abruptly.

"Prisoner, face the wall!"

He turned and pressed his face against the old wallpaper. The escort also pressed their faces to the wall. They stood rigid as a man dressed in a dark-gray suit with a pale face behind rimless glasses walked past at a brisk pace.

Prisoner B was already used to this process. Controller Gibbs insisted that prisoners should not see him but should virtually cease to exist by turning their faces away.

The underlings, marching the prisoner on, disliked this performance.

"Bloody bullshit," said one of them. "Who's he think he is? The Queen?"

The other man responded that things would get even worse when Abraham Ramson came to do his inspection. "You better watch your step then, sonny boy!" he said half-jokingly to Prisoner B, digging him in the ribs. "Ramson's the big cheese—or thinks he is."

The prisoner had seen before that this order of menials, while they performed their duties, were stubbornly set against those in authority over them. Their duties were just a job for them. They went home at six in the evening to wives and kids, and a bottle of beer with a square meal, innocent of ideology.

HE WAS BACK IN HIS CELL. A different room, but much like the previous one. This room had a skylight in its roof, high overhead. The glass had been covered over, but one corner of the fabric covering it had peeled back, allowing in a crack of sunlight. Sunlight lit a small triangular pattern high on one of the walls.

Abraham Ramson . . . Another cause for dread . . .

Lying isolated in the great edifice, he became aware of furtive noises nearby. He raised himself on one elbow and looked about. A cardboard box stood against the near wall. Several mice were busy on top of the box, chewing the wallpaper. He thought to drive them away—but why should he? He tried not to listen to the business of tiny jaws.

Prisoner B went to look at the tiny triangle of light.

He never saw any other prisoner, although he heard their screams. He might otherwise be alone in the world. He knew there were French interrogators and American interrogators, and once there had been a stand-in Polish interrogator.

He was feverish. He imagined that the patch of light was another world where men were free. *Where men were free . . .*

The light faded. He continued to stare at the place it had briefly lit.

It must be night in that other world. It was called Stygia.

He muttered to himself some lines he recalled from a great poem:

> *The Stygian council thus dissolved; and forth*
> *In order came the grand infernal peers;*
> *Midst came their mighty paramount, and seemed*
> *Alone th' antagonist of heaven, nor less*
> *Than hell's dread emperor, with pomp supreme . . .*

A HATCH SET LOW in the cell door opened and a bowl of soup was thrust in. The prisoner knelt and drank from the bowl. The soup was of cabbage, with a ring or two of onion thrown in. He ate greedily, all the while becoming more and more convinced that he knew a world called Stygia, where there was more hope and less harm than in this world.

The ill-tasting soup made him more feverish. He believed himself to be swimming or floating in his wealthy cousin's swimming pool. He was in five feet of water. The sun shone on the back of his head.

He looked down at his shadow on the bottom of the pool. The wavelets he created showed as ripples of light seeming to emanate from his shadow-body. His arms are outspread. He has power. Power resembles strong chords played on a mighty organ.

The emanations carry him onward. He scarcely needs the movement of his arms.

The great ethereal thing is on its way . . . His mind shifts.

The mind is its own place, and in itself
Can make a heaven of hell, a hell of heaven . . .

And he is free upon that other planet. His feet are bare and already walking barren ground. Squadrons of winged insects fly past him. It seemed that Stygia was empty of human beings. He was floating over valleys and mountainous territory, over wide rivers and lucid lakes, over plains and jungles. All he saw living were insects, some of poisonous brightness; others, crawling, of intense blackness.

Many days and nights seemed to pass before he came to a broad, green land which terminated in tall cliffs, standing against a dark, violet sea. There stood the colonial Stygia City.

He circled above it before drifting down and entering the alleys and streets of the strange city. Upon gaining a wide square, he saw before him a grandiose building, presumably the government Center. It had a flat roof, supported at each corner by two large pillars. He moved closer. Vision was bad. At the top of each pillar, carved cherubs nestled, cherubs with huge eyes and fly faces, making light work of pretending to support the roof.

Prisoner B found it difficult to focus his eyes. Hauling himself forward over bare boards, he realized he was looking up at an old grand fireplace. The grate area had been filled in. All that remained was the stone framework, where two ornate pillars, decorated with winged cherubs, supported the shelf of the mantelpiece. The cherubs had plump cheeks and innocent faces. This was the room where he was held captive, a room enclosed in what had once been a grand mansion, now used for inferior and more sinister purposes. Stygia had dissolved to nothing.

Rough hands on his collar pulled him to his feet.

He was walking, dragging his feet, between two armed men, to an interrogation room. They forced him into a chair. A light shone into his eyes. He tried to remember his own name.

Two men entered the room, boots sounding on the bare floorboards. The prisoner saw that the leading man was in uniform; then the light eclipsed his view. The uniformed man sat down on the far side of the table and shuffled some papers. The man who had entered with him stood alertly behind his chair. Then the interrogator spoke, in a deep, slow voice.

"This is where we establish clarity. That is the purpose of this institution. To establish clarity.

"No more fooling around, Prisoner B. We are going to get to the bottom of this matter. You will answer my questions without evasion."

"I have answered all possible questions," said the prisoner. Just to speak was a labor. His mouth was dry and dirty.

"You need to speak distinctly. Guards, water!"

One of the armed men brought up a bucket half full of water and dashed it over the prisoner's face. It did serve to revive him to some extent.

"All right. Your name is Fadhil Abbas Ali, correct?"

"Paul Fadhil Abbas Ali. I am a British citizen."

"What makes you think that?"

"I am second-generation born in London. My father left Uganda as a young man. I was born in Ealing."

"What faith?"

"Well . . . no faith at all, really."

"Answer properly. You are a Muslim. You went to Saudi Arabia last year, visited the city of Qem."

The second man, leaning forward on the table, asked, "What were you planning?"

"Planning nothing. Just on holiday to see where my ancestors came from. Later I went to Israel, where I stayed in the Moriah Plaza Hotel in Tel Aviv. That doesn't make me Jewish."

"Why did you go into the great mosque of Qem?"

"Look, I was a tourist, a British tourist, so I had a look in the famous mosque."

"Who was the man you met there?"

"I didn't meet anyone."

By way of response, the uniformed man produced a glossy photograph from among his papers. He flipped it across the table at the prisoner.

The photo showed the interior of the mosque at Qem. Two men stood together, one in robes, one in shirt and shorts, Western style. Paul recognized himself.

"How did you get this? I don't understand. It's a mock-up, isn't it?"

A gesture from the military man, and one of the guards clouted Prisoner B on the head. The blow almost knocked him off his chair.

"You're lying, you bastard. Who is this guy you met in the mosque? You gave him a slip of paper. What was on the paper?"

"Oh. It's a poor man asking me for alms. I gave him a riyal note." He pushed the photograph away.

Another clout on the head.

"You're lying to me."

"No. It's simply the truth."

"You bastards lie all the time. You don't know truth from lies. What was on that fucking note you passed?"

"It was a riyal note, I tell you. Possibly for ten riyals, I forget." He leaned forward to try to see beyond the bright light, but there was only dazzlement.

"Please, I'm entirely innocent. Let me go! I can't bear this torture."

Both men laughed scornfully. The second man said, "If you want torture, you'll get it all right. We're just questioning you, okay?"

The other man said, "Tomorrow I shall question you about your wife, you bastard. So you'd better think about it."

"Let me go, dammit!"

Now the military man was standing up. "No one gets out of here alive. You're guilty of something or you wouldn't be in here."

"Tell me what country I'm in! Please! They drugged me on the way here."

"You're in the shit. Shit Country." He stamped out, followed by his lackey.

One of the guards clouted Prisoner B over the head again for good measure. Then they frog-marched him out of the room, down the broad corridor, to a room into which they kicked him.

As they turned to leave, he saw the inscription in yellow lettering on the back of their bomber jackets. It read: HOSTILE ACTIVITIES RESEARCH MINISTRY. The words confirmed all his worst fears. Was the kind of brutality to which he was being subjected now incorporated in official government policy? HARM? HARM? Had it really come to this?

Curiously, he tried to exonerate his tormentors. He told himself that it was the so-called terrorists, the Muslim suicide bombers—and their tacit support from the silent Muslim community—which had brought this disgrace on Britain . . .

A curtain of fear had been drawn over the once moderate and modest island.

He heard a key turn in the lock.

His skull was ringing with pain. He sat on the floor with his back against the wall and held his head in his hands.

The ringing continued.

THE BELL HAD RECENTLY been cast. It was supported on the roof of the government Center. It seemed as if everyone on Stygia was making their way to the central square. He, too, was there, going under the name of Fremant. He was weary and broken and the city he came to was gray.

Everyone was mustering in the square, looking expectantly toward the building. A large, bulky man appeared on the balcony and raised his right arm in salute. The crowd roared its acclamation for their leader, Astaroth.

Then spake he. "We were reconstituted before we arrived on Stygia. You know how many light-years we traveled. You know how we travelers became divided into rival sects once we were reconstituted. Those divisions will cease now. This stern planet welcomed us. Indeed, we hope to remain here peacefully, to built a great new civilization, with the support of WAA. But we found the planet overrun by a primitive race, the strange pack of Doglovers.

"Doglovers were the most primitive of any two-legged kind. They built no great buildings, such as this building in which I stand. They built no roads. They had no electronic devices, no mechanical articles, no nothing. They were little better than the hounds that led them about, as the blind are led by guide dogs.

"Who knows what diseases these aliens harbored, unknown to us? With the support and goodwill of distant Earth, of WAA, the Western Armed Alliance, we set about wiping out the Doglovers.

"You were—all of you, of whatever sect—part of that task. One by one our planes and probes were brought down and crashed. We couldn't replace them. We have reason to believe that hordes of locust-like insects choked their jets. Still we fought on. Today, on this great Day of Victory, I am proud to declare that the Doglovers are destroyed, every one of them."

The audience raised a cheer.

"Stygia is a human-owned planet at last, despite the teeming insect world.

"This time is a time of austerity. Tomorrow we must set to work to fill the empty spaces with our own kind, to build farms and houses and roads. But today at least let us celebrate our victory. I do not drink. I abjured alcohol long ago. I am a strict WAAbee. But let this day be an exception. There is free drink for you all."

He raised a clenched fist above his head.

"Drink deep! Be briefly happy! The Doglovers are dead! We humans have crossed the gulfs of space to own, to rule, this Stygian world. We must live austere lives. Austerity must become our faith."

He ceased speaking, and from a thousand throats a cry of triumph rose into the air.

Later, people were reeling about from the drink, eager for the escape to oblivion it provided. Several fell flat on their faces. So Prisoner B found himself, pinned to the ground.

And his consciousness was drawn back to the squalid floor on which he lay, spread like a starfish, facedown, with the chill, dark, old room imprisoning him, throwing back his gasps like malicious whispering. It was as if Stygia never existed; the roars of triumph had turned into the thudding pulse in his head.

At some time in the day or night, a bread roll and more cabbage soup was passed into his prison box. He ate the soup and faded out.

HE WORKS FOR ASTAROTH. He is a guard. He is one of four men responsible for the great leader's safety. He is specifically delegated, in addition, to keep watch on Aster, the leader's woman. It is dark at the center. Aster is melancholy. She does not eat. The circumference of her waist is one-half that of her lord and master, Astaroth. Prisoner B, whose name on Stygia is Fremant, she hates because he serves Astaroth.

Astaroth is a harsh ruler. Many of his eccentricities leave their mark like scars on the city. He creates a currency with notes of four denominations: three stigs, seven stigs, thirteen stigs, and twenty-five stigs. He eats only on odd days. He drinks only water. He banishes all electronic equipment, save only that in the old rusting starship, where research is taking place. He hangs captives, not by the neck, but by an ankle, until they cease struggling and expire.

Astaroth dresses always in black. He is continually meditating. He is a manic-depressive. In starving himself, he starves others.

Fremant is sometimes on duty when Astaroth calls his council together. These arid men, the WAAbees—now the Waabees— have an arid form of belief. The regulations by which the Waabees live include total commitment to the organization; also important are the edicts that there should be no sex before marriage, no private ownership, no fun, no reading, no singing, no bourgeois indulgences such as "kindness" or "understanding"; no affection toward others, including wives. The council was currently debating whether to ban vegetables. Fremant hears but does not hear, for he is just a guard.

Yet sometimes the words of the council get through to him as he stands there, unmoving as a statue. He heard Astaroth declare, "We must be austere on this alien planet or we shall lose our humanity, we shall revert to wild animals. The soil here is poor. Agriculture has yet to prove itself dependable, so we will eat only once a day, at sunset—and then sparingly. We're human, to be sure, in this world riddled with insects. We brought that quality of humanity from the planet Earth, from which we were reconstituted on shipboard. What we did not bring were all the hard-won organizations, the web of relationships between groups of people and nations. Those organizations we must rebuild, even if we kill people in doing so."

WHEN ON DUTY, Fremant sleeps at night on a palliasse spread out before the door to Astaroth's quarters, where Aster also lives. The door is black. Fremant is given a guard's ration, two meals a day, one meal of fish just before dawn, one meal of meat at sunset. The meat is insect "meat" from the dacoim; the fish has been caught within the hour from the great encompassing sea.

Every day at sunup, Fremant exercises, fighting a comrade or else climbing down a cliff and back up again. He is given one free evening per week. At midday every day, he comes before Astaroth and swears his allegiance—unless it is one of those days when the leader's mood is so black he shuts himself in an inner room and will see no one.

"He's not a bad sort of feller. He suffers like the rest of us come off that ship," said Bellamia, brushing back her unruly locks. "We all got somming wrong with us. It's how we were made, I reckon . . ."

Fremant rented a room in Bellamia's house. Whenever Bellamia spoke, a strange aroma issued from her mouth. She grew the herb salack in a patch by her door and chewed it continually. Her two-room house offered little in the way of comfort. It was situated in Caskeg Square, in the shadow of the Center. Almost everyone who lived on the street worked in the Center.

"It's the air, the air's different somehow," Bellamia complained. "Your lungs feel different."

"I don't notice it," he said, unwilling to enter into conversation with the woman. Bellamia was a well-built woman—and, he realized, not as old as he had at first thought her—but wrapped around with a feeling of isolation.

"Then it's me," she said. "I was not properly made. I feel it. Somehow, I feel I am hardly human."

"Don't be silly," he said, not unkindly. After all, she was charging him only half a stig per day for the lodging.

It was generally understood that there was 3 percent more oxygen in the atmosphere than had been the case on distant Earth.

Bellamia kept a green parrot in a cage. When Fremant looked more closely at the creature, it scarcely resembled a bird. It had the compound eyes of an insect, and maxillae instead of a beak. But Bellamia was fond of it in a careless way.

Watching it, he saw the "parrot" did not sing so much as stridulate, rubbing its rear legs briskly together, producing a continuous deep noise, a song much like a cicada's. Bellamia would hum her own tune to this gentle noise.

Everyone appeared poor in Stygia City. The men lived in threadbare, patched clothes. The poverty extended to their speech patterns. Fremant gradually became aware of how impoverished was their vocabulary. The disintegration on the long space journey had attenuated speech; and the sparse environment of Stygia encouraged no replenishment of words.

"How old is Astaroth?" Fremant asked his landlady.

"He'd be about sixty, give or take a year or two." She breathed out her aroma.

Fremant was surprised. He had yet to adjust to the Stygian year, which was only 291 Earth days long, and thus only four-fifths of a terrestrial year.

"His old wife, Ameethira, must be seventy, but you never see her about," said Bellamia. She went *tsk tsk*, and shook her head gloomily.

At noon, the shadow of a brewery where buskade was brewed passed across Bellamia's house. Opposite the brewery stood a church, the Church of Cosmonauts. Its doleful bell rang every seventh day. Many penitents met there, to complain and condole.

STYGIA CITY WAS in the temperate zone of the planet. The people who lived under Astaroth's rule, whose components had traveled from Earth in refrigerated vats, lived in humble dwellings clustered around squares. In these squares, life of a sort continued. At food shops here, music of a sort was heard, issuing from a single instrument; people could eat in the open air. Wandering through one square, in his free evening, Fremant met a woman he greatly liked.

This woman, like all Stygia's women except for old crones, went hooded and masked when outside her home. Fremant never saw her face. She told him her name was Duskshine. They held hands and he gazed at her fingers, since he could not see her eyes. The fingers were slender, the nails pale and pointed.

Duskshine was slightly built. He was amused by the way she gestured as she spoke, her frail hands fluttering before her as if with a suppressed eloquence of their own. He found it an attractive characteristic.

The courtship went slowly. Fremant was able to spend so little time with Duskshine. The protocol was against love and lovemaking. Also, there were periods when Stygia underwent Dimoffs, as they were called, when a "shawl" of dark matter came between the planet and its sun. This Shawl spread across the sky in hundreds of small rocky fragments, black and forbidding, cutting off light and heat, so that people kept within their homes and said nothing, lying about and waiting for goodness to return to the world.

Following the fashion, Fremant flung himself down on his rug and attempted to sleep. Nightmare filled his sleeping mind. At one moment he seemed to be tramping for hours across a desert. Then he was trying to lick the flesh of a woman who stank from a septic fistula. A gigantic man was attempting to pull him away.

Half-waking, Fremant found himself again dragged to his feet. A hood was tied over his head and he was taken before another interrogator. To be totally deprived of sight was a terror in itself.

"You lived with a whore?" he was asked.

"No." He was led to a backless chair, terrified. "For Allah's sake, tell me where I am!"

A kind of chuckle from the interrogator. "You're far from home, prisoner. You're in Uzbekistan, well away from EU law . . ."

"Not Syria?"

"You heard what I said."

"Spare me. Have pity on me! Please tell me the date and where we are. I—I'm lost. Please! I have personality problems."

He produced a much-folded letter from a psychiatrist he had visited at the Maudesley Institute which suggested that his sense of isolation, of not knowing where he was, or when, reinforced a dissociative disorder, causing alternative personalities to emerge. A course of treatment was recommended.

The interrogator glanced at the letter, then refolded it and tore it to pieces. He tapped a note into his laptop.

"You're having a stay in Hotel California, and it's fucking Christmas!" The questioner then repeated his question. "You lived with a whore?"

"I live with my wife. She is a good woman, not at all a whore."

"She is a white woman. To marry you, she must be a whore."

The interrogation chamber held an evil stink, a cocktail of fear, blood, sweat, and malice. There were no windows to open for fresh air. Fresh air represented freedom.

He was struck in the ribs by a club and gave a cry of pain.

"Tell me her name."

"You must know her name."

Again a blow to his ribs.

"Name, you bastard."

"Doris."

"She was your cover while you planned the destruction of the state."

"She is my wife, whom I love. I planned no destruction. I lived the life of an ordinary Englishman, except I was Muslim."

"You shit, you married a decent Englishwoman under false pretenses. Admit it . . . Fucking admit it!"

"No, no, it's not true. Doris and I love—arrrhh! Oh!"

The blow landed across his spine. One of the guards brought up his club and, jerking Prisoner B's head back, pressed the club against his windpipe, so that he could scarcely breathe. Blood surged before his eyes in the darkness of his hood. He scarcely heard what the interrogator was saying.

"You made the bitch turn Muslim, didn't you?"

"It was"—he could hardly speak—"voluntary."

"Your whore hates you. She says you met with members of Hamas when you were in the mosque at Qem."

"No, no, not true . . ."

"Oh yes, it fucking well is true. Listen!"

The interrogator was playing back a recording. Prisoner B heard his wife's cries of pain. She begged them not to apply the burning electric currents again, not *there* . . . Then she screamed again. In a faint voice, she said the words, *I hate Paul.* She was prompted, "And he met with members of Hamas?" . . . *Oh, yes, yes,* she said. She was in tears now. *He met with members of*

Hamas. "Where did this take place? It was in the mosque at Qem and elsewhere." . . . *Oh, all right, it was in the mosque at Qem.* "And elsewhere, you cow!" *Yes, okay, and elsewhere. Oh, Paul, I'm so sorry . . . Owwww . . . Not again, please . . .*

Her cries of pain were switched off. Amid his dismay he thought, She could not help betraying me. The pain was too much for her. I understand, Doris, poor sweet darling. I do understand. He tried to believe the recording was a fake. He did not think the voice was his wife's. All was uncertain.

"You can stay here and think about it, you little fucker."

The guards strapped him to the chair, with ties around his ankles and chest, securing him tightly until every breath was a labor. He heard the interrogator walk off. The guards remained. Although they were silent, he felt their presence. One of them rubbed the stubble on his cheek, the other scratched his balls.

Prisoner B waited, trembling with fear in anticipation of the next punishment, although little could be worse than listening to his wife in pain. The knowledge that they were torturing Doris as well as him was unbearable, a poison to the system. He thought what a little worm he was. Time passed. He could not estimate how much.

His grip on himself had loosened. He had entered a new region, where things were probably not what they seemed, where distinctions between day and night had been lost. No longer were there normal patterns of meals. Wet and dry, clean and dirty, truth and lies, all had been terminally disheveled.

His head throbbed noisily. Gradually, pressure in his bladder increased. He tried to deflect all thought of the need to urinate. Perhaps they intended that he should piss himself, thus adding to his degradation.

Blackness inside the hood was complete. It was hard to breathe. He feared a heart attack.

It was a relief when a guard grabbed his arm, saying, "All right, get up."

As the straps were released and he struggled to his feet, he gasped, "I need the toilet, please."

He knew it was a mistake. Something like a chuckle in the man's voice sounded as he said, "You'll have to wait a bit . . ."

They stood him against a wall. He was still in the interrogation room. His hood was removed. He gasped in the fresher air, feeling his face drip sweat. The faces of the guards were familiar. One, the taller of the two, with odd, reddened cheeks standing out like buns and a nose little more than a blob; the other, younger, with a long, dim, sallow face, expressionless, with narrow dark eyes.

Prisoner B felt that the older of the two was not sadistic, merely doing his job within the cruel machine of interrogation and the dictates of the old CIA "Kubark Manual." He supposed this man was English. With the other, it was hard to tell.

He addressed the older man, as possibly the less cruel of the two.

"Oh, please, the toilet. I'm bursting."

"Hang on."

"I'm bursting. Is this Guantánamo? Are we in Guantánamo?"

The younger guard, the one with the sallow face, punched him in the stomach.

"Don' ask questions."

They led him into the corridor. Such was his agony, he could not stop himself. Rather than wet himself, he wrenched out his penis and urinated in a burst against the wall. The liquid poured from him, splashing the guards. The relief was so immense, he scarcely felt their blows, until a fist, catching him behind the ear, sent him reeling.

He fell, still urinating, and lay there sobbing in a pool of his own piss.

TWO

A WHILE LATER, he realized he was swimming in a small lake. He had to adjust to the reality of it. Warm though the water was, cold was in the air and a speckled darkness spread overhead. The Shawl was passing, that sheet of dust and debris in near-space which brought Dimoff. He and Duskshine were taking advantage of the Dimoff to cross the lake and visit some associates of hers.

Duskshine still wore her all-concealing veil. She swam confidently beside him. Eventually, his feet touched shingle. He vaguely made out a shoreline with small hills beyond, although all was featureless at this period. When Fremant began to tread sand, he turned to assist the woman.

Their clothes dripping, they gained the shore. Once out of the water, the cold got to them. A challenge was called ahead. She answered. A man came up to them, leading them to a path. Some men came close, silent, showing no light. He felt their hostility.

He was intimidated. The long, coarse grass of Stygia brushed their legs. They were guided to a hut behind a ridge and ushered in. The men followed, closing the door. They negotiated an insect-screen. Then a lamp was lit. They were in a long room, furnished with benches and tables.

To one side stood an iron stove. A woman opened a door in its belly and warmth filtered into the room. Duskshine and Fremant were brought nearer to it, in order to help them dry off. They were glad of it and stood shivering, hands extended to the flames. Her fingers were long and pointed.

A tall old man with a mane of silver hair came forward and clutched the hands of both of them in welcome.

"My name is Habander. I am one of the Clandestine Order. We welcome you here. But we need to search you."

While the search was in process, Habander raised an interrogatory eyebrow at the girl.

Duskshine prompted Fremant to introduce himself.

"He's here secretly," she said, her gesticulating hands also trying to explain the situation. "He is one of four of Astaroth's guards. He must return to the Center before the Shawl passes. Astaroth shuts himself up all alone when it is Dimoff. He comes out afterward and checks that all is as it should be."

"How do you know he's alone? Completely alone?" Habander asked. "And the—er, the wife?"

The hands fluttered. "Ameethira? They are rarely together . . ."

She sighed and looked away.

Tension mounted in Fremant. There was something here he did not understand.

Words of welcome came from the throats of many of the men and women assembled in the long, drab room. They had recognized Duskshine. Fremant looked about him. The place reeked of sweat and food and piss. The men here appeared anxious, not of fighting quality. Much like himself, in fact.

"What's all the secrecy about?" Fremant asked.

Habander replied. He had come with his Clandestine companions to Stygia on the starship. The captain, Captain Calex, had been a wise and compassionate man, a great thinker. He had hated the confusions and terror of Earth cultures and had sought out the planet Stygia like a pilgrim, to build a more just world. Many of those who voyaged, as essence, on the ship felt as he did. Many, but not all.

When the colonists had been reconstituted and the ship finally made landfall, Captain Calex gave a moving speech, according to Habander.

"He said that we would build a single gentle culture, without the divisions that troubled Earth, with its poisonous history. Our first big effort must be to make friends with the native peoples who lived on this world. There must be no sexual reproduction until we have peace. Peace is paramount. They are strange to us—he said that—but we must face that strangeness and prepare. Any remaining weapons must be destroyed—"

While Habander was reporting on this noble speech, with an eloquence of his own, Fremant was saying to himself with equal passion, "Who are these crazy people? I prefer working in the Center. Overbearing though Astaroth is, he is at least a reasonable man. Well, with some eccentricities, and of course that poisonous creed. Why did I allow Duskshine to bring me here to this gang of loonies?

"Why do I trust this bitch when I can't even see her face? Why do I always play subordinate roles in life? What a pathetic loser I am! And then these nightmare episodes I have, when I seem to be a prisoner somewhere and have to undergo a series of tortures . . . I'm in my twenties still—I should see someone about all this. Habander is probably another figment of my hallucinations."

But Habander was concluding by saying that even before the captain finished his address, a figure jumped on the platform holding a knife.

The crowd watching gave a great cry. They recognized Astaroth as the attacker. On the ship, after reconstitution, Astaroth had been the leader of the clique known as the Waabees, which had developed in opposition to the Calex party. The Calex party, in the furtherance of peace, had destroyed all weapons on the ship. Astaroth alone had concealed a weapon.

The knife came down. Captain Calex raised an arm against his attacker. The knife plunged into his heart. He fell at once.

Many in the crowd gasped in horror, while others of the Waabee party cheered. The assassin shouted, "I am Astaroth! You'll get to know me better! This dead man misled you all. He was the fool captain who destroyed our weapons. These natives here, these primitive dog-owners, are going to rise and kill us all if we don't make a show of strength. We are a mere handful of humanity. There are who-knows-how-many millions of *them*! We must fight them, and no nonsense about it!"

So it was, said Habander, that Astaroth had come to rule with his stern ascetic creed, calling himself the All-Powerful. He claimed to have secret orders from distant Earth, in particular from WAA. It was on these orders, he claimed, that he and his men began the killing of natives. Task forces were sent out from the city.

"We Clandestines seek to overthrow Astaroth. We want to make peace with the natives—those who survive."

Habander fell silent. He then spoke quietly to Fremant. "So this woman you call Duskshine brought you here. We know who she is. We know you are a guard of Astaroth's. Why would we trust you?"

Looking into Habander's face, Fremant felt some compassion. Here was a man wanting to be liked—in fact, a loser. A loser, yet correct in rejecting Astaroth's policy of genocide.

"In another life, I was peaceful, Habander. I was a writer. I wrote comic novels. The only job I could get here was as a guard. I assure you I have no affection for Astaroth."

Several Clandestines had gathered to listen, suspiciously, to the conversation. One of them, bearded and as pale as paper, now asked, challengingly, "What is the name of your god?"

"Believe me, I'm too poor to afford a god."

The group muttered to itself at this answer. "So what about god?" Fremant asked, impatiently. "Who is your god?"

The pale man now pushed himself forward, pointing a grimy finger at Fremant. "We have all been reconstituted. It is a resurrection. So we know our god is great and rules this insect-ridden world. His name may not be spoken—certainly not to you, a stranger."

Habander spoke reprovingly. "Please do not offend this man whose help we need." Turning to Fremant, he said, in a lowered tone, "We do not dare mention the name of our god in case the insect world hears of it and so takes power over us. But you must believe, our god is great and rules the clouds and the seas of Stygia."

Fremant was tired of all the oratory and wished to get back to the Center before the Shawl had passed.

"What's all this to me?" he asked contemptuously.

Duskshine touched his arm. "We need you to kill Astaroth," she said. Her frail little hands made a downward chopping motion.

The small community started clapping and cheering.

Fremant took a deep breath. "Haven't you Clandestines got the guts to kill Astaroth yourselves?" Later he reflected that it was at this moment that he ceased to be a loser and became something more formidable. He had fallen into the servitude of a man he hated and despised—yes, and feared. Astaroth was a dictator. Yes, it would purge his soul to assassinate him.

A small bald man with a meager mustache answered him. "Three of our number tried to kill the hated Astaroth the All-Powerful in the past few months. All died trying. But you get close to him in your duties all the time."

"Yes, for that reason you are ideal," another chimed in. "Ideal!"

"Okay, *you* deal if you like, but *I* don't play cards," Fremant said, but no one present understood puns. "What's your secret god doing about all this?"

"Please," said Duskshine, clutching his arm. "You are so brave, Fremant, dearest. Strike for being free of tyranny. Then I will be yours."

"All right. I'll do it. I will kill him. I need no nameless god! I'm no coward."

He was made to swear on a homemade wooden sword. Anger rose in him. These poor homeless people hid out on this island. Although Stygia was no Paradise, they should be able to lead quiet, ordinary lives. That might come about if he killed Astaroth. In his mind, he saw himself doing the deed—and winning glory for it . . .

He and the hooded woman swam back across the lake. All the way, ferocity boiled up in him. As they climbed the shore, he demanded to know why she had not warned him what he was in for. She said she trusted him but needed secrecy. She loved him.

"Love? Love? You don't even trust me to see your face!"

"It's the rule here, dearest . . . You know Astaroth insists women go veiled."

"Astaroth!" *Another Ramson* . . . Ramson, Ramson? Who was . . . But the thought darted away like a small fish among reeds.

In a rage, he flung her down on the bank and sat astride her. He tugged and tugged at her hood, tightly tied about her neck. He ripped it off, to stare down at the face, gray in the pallid light, of Aster, the wife or the mistress of Astaroth.

"You, you brazen bitch? You'd kill your man for love—not for principle? What sort of a woman are you?"

"Let me go! I hate him, I hate the bully—you have no idea how greatly!" Her face became a mask of loathing.

"You vile scheming insect! You tricked me into this! Why couldn't you be honest?"

"You don't know what I—"

"You don't know what the word *honest* means! I'll show you what it means!"

He stifled her words. He tore off her clothes. She fought him in silence, trying to bite and scratch as they rolled in mud. Still he held her down, growling with rage and lust, finally ripping off her undergarments, tearing them from her legs. The animal scents of her body maddened him. He forced his flesh into her, with a savagery and bitterness that held no joy—a victor's act. Aster ceased struggling and gave a groan between pain and pleasure, though her face remained distorted with anger.

The Shawl slid over to the western sky, revealing a sickly dawn.

Not speaking, they made their way back to the Center, she clutching her torn clothes, sobbing as she went.

ONCE THEY GAINED THE STREETS, they parted without a word, only a bitter backward look. In his billet, clothes still wet, he flung himself down on his mattress, to dive as into a cold, dark pool of exhaustion.

He was coming before the All-Powerful when the nightmare overtook him, and the two guards were pulling him to his feet. The room was in darkness, made more shadowy by the lantern one of the guards had set on the floor while manhandling him.

"Treat for you today. Extra-special interrogator here. Better watch your step, matey!"

"Who is he?"

"Santa Claus. Get moving and don't ask questions."

Prisoner B was helped along the corridor, his feet sliding on the floor. The floor of this corridor was covered by a coarse carpeting of sorts, perhaps coconut matting; it was not the usual corridor down which he had been dragged before. They propelled him into a room he had not been in previously. He was strapped into a chair, and his head was wedged so that he was unable to move it. The older guard brought up two wires from a nearby machine and attached them with a clamp to his temples, one on one side, one on the other.

Then they stepped back and sat on a dusty sofa, to wait. They muttered to one another in tones of complaint. The prisoner heard one say to the other, "After all, the Yanks are the only friends we've got."

"What about the French?"

"The *French*? Ferget it!"

Part of the terror regimen was to keep prisoners waiting for whatever was to come. Dread and the imagination worked further to undo them.

Slowly, Prisoner B took in his surroundings. He was waiting in a small part of what had once been a much bigger, grander room. Partitions cut off all but a small portion of the old room. Through one partition, a man's voice could be heard saying, sobbing, "I admit I did it. I know I did it. I admit I did it. I must have done it. I didn't realize. I admit I did it. Spare me," over and over. The repetition drained the words of emotion.

One feature of the magnificent scale on which life had been lived in this grand mansion was a bust set in an alcove in the wall at just above eye level. The bust was surrounded by a frame of carved stone laurel leaves. The bust itself was of white marble. It commemorated an elderly man with curled hair and a prominent patrician nose. The dead lips were pursed. His stony gaze, directed down at the occupants of the room, expressed contempt.

Below the bust was his name and his titles. He was a general, a leader of armies, who had been knighted.

Now a spider's web was woven across the raised lettering. It was clear that he had been responsible for the deaths of many men—both the enemy and his own compatriots, who had had no choice but to follow him. For this carnage he had been celebrated by a grateful nation.

The prisoner regarded this relic of the good old days with a dull wonder. It could be, he speculated, that this bust indicated that he was imprisoned in a building, palatial and grand, which had once served as the British Embassy in some foreign capital. In Baghdad? In Damascus? Someone had told him that he had been moved to Syria. The speculation was far from encouraging.

He could not recall how he had arrived in this place. All was uncertainty. In his befuddled brain, he wondered if all men were made of stone.

A LARGE, HEAVY MAN entered the room by a rear door, accompanied by a small, scurrying type of lackey. The big man walked to a chair and stood waiting, staring ahead as blankly as the bust behind him, while his inferior placed a cushion on the seat, officiously adjusting it. The big man sat himself down, placing a book on the table before him.

He looked across at Prisoner B with a toadlike, expressionless stare. He began to speak in a deep voice, with elaborate politeness.

"Good morning. My name is Abraham Ramson. I hold the rank of Paramount Government Inspector of the Western Armed Alliance and occupy a senior position in the American Punishment Section investigating hostile activities in the world. I am well known on both sides of the Atlantic as a military judge, famed for holding the lives of many villains in my hands. My aim is to function as a terror of the terrorists. I have prosecuted many famous cases and, although justice interests me, over and above justice I value the continued survival of Western civilization as of maximum import for the culture of this world, as the greatest bastion of enlightened law and behavior on this planet, certainly in comparison with the degenerate and superstitious tribalism prevalent in the Middle East. As a Muslim, you will be aware that we in the West—"

Here the prisoner interrupted to protest that he was not of the Muslim faith.

"You will shut the fuck up, you scumbag, while I am speaking!

"—we in the West have a distaste for Sharia law as well as for many Islamic rules of behavior, from the circumcision of women to the indoctrination of ignorant youths into a form of religion which is in most respects long obsolete and degrading.

"You know what Wahhabism is, Prisoner B?"

B was startled to be suddenly expected to speak. "Wahhabism? Yes, I have heard of it . . ."

"It is a hateful, archaic creed which destroys relationships and withers everything creative. We must fight it before it destroys us, like deathwatch beetles destroy sturdy oak beams. The slaves of Wahhab have the deathwatch habit of infiltrating and endeavoring to destroy the decent and law-abiding cultures into which you have inserted yourselves; together with the cowardly resort of suicide bombing.

"All this I tell you to make my position clear. You must understand, before I question you, that if your answers are unsatisfactory in any way, you will receive a series of electric shocks of increasing severity. So, Prisoner B, question number one: What were your motives when you wrote this subversive novel entitled *Pied Piper of Hament*?"

All of this speech, designed to be deliberately offensive, was spoken rapidly without pause in a deep, cultured, American voice.

Prisoner B, disconcerted, hesitated.

"I have to explain, sir, that I was born in London, in the borough of Ealing, and I have always considered myself an Englishman, even to the extent of—"

"I will remind you that I asked you why you wrote this pernicious novel."

"Sir, I was under the impression I was English and so I wrote this novel in a comical satiric style, hoping to amuse people."

"And what sort of people did you hope it would amuse?"

"Ordinary literate people, I suppose."

"You suppose?" A frown creased the broad brow of Abraham Ramson. "You mean Muslims, naturally?"

"No, sir, the British reading public in general."

"You are contradicting me?" Abraham Ramson gestured with his right hand. A man working beyond Prisoner B's limited line of sight threw a small lever. The electric shock burned between Prisoner B's temples, a flash of lightning, of unbearable pain. Then it was gone, leaving the prisoner fearing that some part of his brain had been burned out. He was immediately craven.

"Oh, sir, no more of that, I beg. I do not intend to contradict. I admit I did it. I didn't realize it. I have every respect . . . I'm confused. I'm starved of sleep. I don't even know what country I'm in. I wrote my novel in good faith. You see, I admire the comic novels of P. G. Wodehouse, that most—"

"You are in Uzbekistan, prisoner, for special interrogation. Now, question number two: Why was your novel translated into a foreign tongue and published in Tehran, an indication of its subversive pro-Islamic nature?"

"Uzbekistan, sir? I don't understand. I—"

The hand gesture again. Again the searing pain, more intense this time, as the world filled with an agonizing blindness.

"Answer the question. Why was your stinking, corrupt novel published in Tehran?"

"Sir, I had no control over where my novel was published. It was also published in the United States of America, and—"

Again the hand gesture. Again the shock. Again he heard his own screams.

"Why in Tehran, prisoner?"

"No more shocks, no more, I beg you. I am trying—trying to answer . . . Really . . . I can't . . . I was told that my novel was published by a small dissenting company in Tehran, to prove that writings by a Muslim could be published in a Western country."

"You are saying you are or are not a Muslim?"

"Well, sir, please, sir—" He heard his own voice blubbering like a schoolchild. "My name is Paul Fadhil Abbas Ali, but I am not a believer."

"You lie, you scumbag! Tell me what fine line divides a Muslim from a pro-Muslim? Are you not pro-Muslim?"

"Well, yes. No. No, in many cases not, but of course—"

Again the hand gesture. Again the blaze at the temples. Again the screams. The tongue burning in the mouth.

Ramson was saying in a casual manner that the prisoner had planned to kill the British prime minister.

"I could never bring myself to kill another person . . ."

Abraham Ramson ignored the remark. Spreading open the prisoner's novel on the table, he flattened its pages with a meaty hand.

Ramson's eyebrows came together as he spoke. "I shall read a passage on page fifty-three of your poisonous creation. 'They were laughing together as they walked through the park, where no one could overhear their jokes. Harry said, "What we need to do is blow up the prime minister. That would solve our problems." "I can see it now," Celina said, laughing. "Bits of him spread all over Downing Street." '

"Is that or is that not an incitement to murder?"

The prisoner was aghast. "How can you take it seriously? They're pretty drunk, these characters, Lina and the others. They're fooling around. Many of my friends just found that passage funny."

"Funny?" The question exploded from his lips. "Bits of the prime minister spread all over Downing Street? Funny? A cause for amusement? You regard that as funny? To me it suggests a preparation for assassination, a suicide bombing, doesn't it?"

"No, really, it is funny, a British sort of a joke. A Monty Python sort of joke . . ."

"You are a traitor, prisoner. A bastard and an asshole."

"Yes, sir, oh yes, I am a fool, but—but really no traitor—and I regret I wrote that passage since things have become so bad. I mean the recent—well, the recent terrorist attacks getting worse. But an innocent fool, sir, please believe—Ohhhhh!"

Again, the gesture, the shock, the agony, the blindness.

"No one is innocent in this world. You abused the privilege of living in a civilized country. Take this wretch away, guards," said Abraham Ramson.

As they dragged the prisoner off, he called back, "Please, sir, please repatriate me to England. I don't deserve this punishment!"

"Shut up, you prick," said one of the guards. But in a good-humored way.

AFTER CONDUCTING THIS BRIEF INTERROGATION, Inspector Abraham Ramson walked at his steady pace down the corridor to the washroom. He fitted tightly into his neat suit. His leather shoes shone. On the way to the washroom, passing a pile of rubbish, he was met by Algernon Gibbs, the controller of the establishment, a wispy little man with designer stubble and rimless eyeglasses. His dyed dark hair was parted exactly in the middle of his skull.

"Er, everything going well, Inspector?" he asked, with a forced smile.

Without pausing in his stride, Ramson said, "Prisoner B says he is a fool and I believe him. He *is* a fool."

Gibbs gave an uncertain titter. He did not like the burly Ramson and regretted that higher authorities had sent him here to interfere with the working of the organization. He followed Ramson into the washroom.

White tiles and mirrors on the walls. Stains on the floor. Controller Gibbs slyly regarded himself in the mirrors. He approved of what he saw, contrasting his own pale hands— "refined," as he thought of them—with the big, brutish knuckles of his visitor.

"Who've we got next?" Ramson asked, as he removed his jacket and hung it on a hook. "Someone worthy of a proper interrogation, I hope. Someone with a heap more nastiness in him, eh?" As he rolled up his sleeves, Gibbs brought out a packet of cigarettes and offered one to the American.

"You're not still smoking those filthy things?" Ramson said, by way of refusal.

"The burden of office, you know. Sometimes the prisoners . . ."

His voice was drowned as Ramson turned on the tap and water came gushing forth. Repeatedly jabbing the liquid soap button, he worked up a fine lather, energetically turning his hands about and about, soaping them up to his hairy wrists.

"I'll take a look at the records. I have concluded that you are wasting your time on this guy B, Algy."

"The records are of course available, Inspector." Gibbs spoke stiffly, irritated by the familiarity of the abbreviation—even the use—of his first name.

Ramson grabbed two paper towels and dried himself vigorously, ignoring the smaller man. "Help me on with my jacket, will you?"

In the record room, he sat down in front of a computer and tapped in the coded password.

"Would you care for a drink? A lager, or something stronger?" Gibbs inquired.

"I don't drink, Algy. I would have thought you knew that well enough."

"A glass of mineral water, then? Or something even stronger? A lemonade?" A thin smile.

"Mineral water's fine. Fizzy. With ice, if you have it. Plenty of ice."

Going to the door, Gibbs summoned an assistant, saying quietly, "A glass of mineral water for our guest. No ice."

Ramson pulled up Prisoner B's file.

The screen revealed an extensive record of Prisoner B's antecedents.

His grandfather had left the state of Hyderabad in India to serve as an indentured laborer in British-held Uganda. He worked in a copper mine. He had married, and his wife delivered three sons and a daughter. One of these sons became B's father.

This son was clever. He established a small grocery store in Kampala, the Ugandan capital. The store catered not just to the 18 percent of the population that was Muslim but to all Ugandans, irrespective of their faith. He was successful and moved to a larger store at a better site, on Gladstone Street. There he attracted wealthy white patronage.

Still a young man, he part-funded the building of a local mosque, thus incurring the enmity of a British official with conflicting property interests. B's father soon moved to Britain, where he was again successful, founding the store Beezue in Queensway. His racehorse Thark won the 1997 Derby. In his forties, he married an Englishwoman, Gloriana Harbottle, by whom he had a son (B) and a daughter.

Gloriana had written children's stories, which influenced B. His father maltreated him. Beating, shutting in cupboards were recorded.

Abraham Ramson gave a grim chortle. "So they called him 'Insane Hussein' at school . . . It says here that while shut in one of these cupboards he renounced the Muslim faith.

"Ever been shut in a cupboard for a week, Algy? It makes a difference, let me tell you."

Gibbs sighed. "No doubt. What else?"

Ramson turned to the screen again.

"In his teens, B left home and lived for some time with a woman hairdresser, Janet Stevens. He underwent psychoanalysis for his various insecurities. The course was funded by a league to help recent immigrants. His first story, 'Eve in the Evening,' was published in *Granta* and he was taken up by a literary crowd. He married Doris McGinty, an Irishwoman with literary ambitions. It is claimed that she helped him write his comic novel, *Pied Piper of Hament*. The novel betrays little of B's origins."

Having read these notes and checked the dates, Ramson looked up from the screen.

"Well, it's a British story. You Brits were too lenient on these guys. You see, you let the shits in, then they betray us."

Gibbs, standing behind him smoking, agreed. "We've been too liberal by half."

Glaring up from his chair, Ramson looked at a point over Gibbs's shoulder to deliver his next comment. "You do a lot of things by halves, Algy. Interrogation methods are strictly amateur—nothing improved since World War Two—"

"The gov'ment is extremely parsimonious with our finances—"

"Not enough psychological leverage used. It leaves no mark on the suspect. You should read up about our various methods. Fake drowning. The waterboard. That's excellent—fake drowning. Then again, you don't have properly trained staff here, men who like the work and know how to apply it."

Ramson rose from his chair. He had left his mineral water untouched. "However, this guy, he's nothing. All flimflam. Let him go. Kick him out. You're wasting your time with him, Algy."

But Gibbs was pursuing his own line of thought. He dropped the stub of his cigarette and crushed it out on the floor with his boot. "I'd nuke the lot of them, given the chance."

As they made for the door together, Ramson said, with the usual note of contempt in his voice, "Yeah, I'd certainly nuke a good many of 'em. Trouble is, nuking is not very selective. It's not WAA policy, okay? It's all or nothing with nuking, Algy."

"So much the better."

IT WAS STILL DARK. His head still ached. He listened to his own sobbing, wondering where it came from.

"Shut up, will you?" said one of the four guards, shaking Fremant's shoulder. "What's wrong with you? Yelling in your sleep, you woke me up." His name was Tunderkin and he lay on his palliasse next to Fremant. His face was broad and honest, with a scar on the left cheek. He had long blond hair and big muscles. He was in his teens.

Fremant sat up, dazed. "I was having a nightmare."

"Have a quiet nightmare next time." Tunderkin settled himself down for more sleep. Fremant remained awake, feeling chilled to his very core.

He sat up, clutching his knees. His past was lost to him, his future problematic.

To assassinate the leader, Astaroth, would not be overwhelmingly difficult. However, when he plunged in the dagger, the other three guards would, without a doubt, set on him. The question he asked himself was: Could he persuade the other guards that killing the All-Powerful was a good thing? They might have no liking for Astaroth, but he provided their livelihood. Two of them, not young Tunderkin, but Imascalte and Cavertal, were married with children.

He spoke to them in cautious terms. Tunderkin once ventured the remark that Astaroth had mistreated his woman, Aster. The other guards had merely frowned.

The days went by and he did nothing. When Aster was near, she simply averted her gaze from him. As Fremant got to understand the workings of the Center better, he saw that there were plenty of potential contenders for the leadership, were Astaroth to die: two men in particular, Desnaith and Safelkty, competitors and rivals; Desnaith all outward charm, Safelkty heavy and moody, a promoter of science.

The question arose in Fremant's mind: Would the community be any happier under one of these men, supposing Astaroth were dead? And supposing they, too, were killed—there would be others, just as avid for power. Including Habander. And so the Clandestines' assassination plan began to appear to him too simplistic.

There was always an inherent threat in all power being in the hands of one man—any man.

While Fremant did nothing but his duties, while he mulled over these problems, a note was handed to him. It read only, "Strike within ten days, or we strike you. C."

The Clandestines were growing impatient. He tried to tell himself that they were not contenders. He was safe while he remained in the Center.

A STIR OF EXCITEMENT ran through the Center one day. First, Astaroth appeared in a night-black cloak, a band of followers behind him, similarly dressed. A military-type band practiced in the courtyard. Fish and a dozen local dacoims were brought in to be baked over glowing embers. A reception was in preparation. Guards were given extra duties.

Late in the afternoon, a posse of men riding the local variety of horse appeared from the direction of the hills, to be greeted by fanfares. A crowd had gathered, with many women, hooded and veiled, among them. They ran to greet the riders, their pale hands upraised.

The riders brought with them a wheeled cage. They stopped outside the Center, to be greeted formally by Astaroth, flanked by his guards, including Fremant.

Astaroth spoke. The crowd fell silent. He praised the returning expedition. The leader of the expedition, a tall, dignified man by the name of Essanits, with white stubble patching his jawline, then bowed to Astaroth. With a nod of permission from the All-Powerful, he addressed the crowd.

"We are glad to return to Stygia City. We come bringing victory with us. Ours has been a bloody task. I speak for most of my men when I say we carried out our duties with heavy hearts — the task of killing off our enemies, the Dogovers, or Doglovers as we used to know them. We slaughtered them when and where we tracked them down. I have to tell you that not one Dogover now remains alive on the face of Stygia."

At this announcement, cheers rang out from the crowd.

Essanits, with a hint of irony in his voice, continued: "So you can now sleep easy in your beds. For us, in some cases we now have to endure a time of regretting, of penitence, because mass slaughter, even of aliens, is never pleasant. It goes against the God-given human conscience, the commandment to preserve life. While we killed off all the dogs we could find, we have brought back some prisoners—five of the Dogover tribe for you to see. Bromheed, bring the prisoners out for inspection."

As ordered, the warrior called Bromheed opened up the door of the wheeled cage. Using a stick, he made the five prisoners emerge from the cage into the square. They stood in a forlorn group, none higher than a ten-year-old human child. They had milky-white faces and hair of the same color. Fremant studied them with interest. Poor little creatures, he thought. Their bodies were entirely cloaked in a sort of furry material, down to the ankles. Their feet were bare.

They stood motionless before the crowd, their heads lowered.

The onlookers muttered uneasily to one another. Then, recognizing the helplessness of those small folk they had decided were their enemies, they began to laugh—to laugh scornfully, Fremant thought as he listened, not only at the Dogovers but at their own fears.

This cruel noise affected the prisoners. They turned to one another, forming a small ring, linking arms over each other's shoulders, putting their heads together.

Essanits swore a holy oath and ran to break up the ring. But too late. The prisoners collapsed, slowly, to sprawl in an entangled mass at Essanits's feet.

Essanits fell to his knees and pulled one of the childlike folk to him. Its head lolled foolishly on its shoulders. Like the others, it was dead.

He laid the corpse gently down before turning to address Astaroth and the watching crowd. "Oh, sadness! We have witnessed this strange occurrence before. These little people, rather than bear disgrace, can will themselves to die. It is an uncanny, alien talent which we humans do not possess.

"I deeply regret my part in this . . . in all this . . ."

Tears of compassion glittered in his eyes as he spoke.

"Be a man, Essanits, damn you!" exclaimed the All-Powerful. "Whatever the cause, these weaklings committed suicide. Did not these feeble little creatures deserve to die? We would have killed them anyway." He turned on his heel and strode back into the Center, closely followed by his guards. Meanwhile, the crowd had fallen silent. Conditions on Stygia were such that many had ended their own lives.

The scene had made a deep impression on many, not least on Fremant. The people assembled in the square drifted away, in silence or muttering uneasily to one another.

A scientific man, by name Tolsteem, one of Astaroth's few researchers, stopped Essanits in the hall.

"Excuse me, sir, I heard you refer to willed death as uncanny. That is not necessarily the case. In the human frame, the constant beating of the heart is part of our autonomic nervous system. I surmise that in the case of the Dogovers, so called, their hearts are controlled by parasympathetic nerves which can slow the heart so severely it can cause death. Inhibition of the heart is known in humans and—"

"What does all this nonsense mean?" Essanits demanded. "They died, didn't they?"

"You miss my point, sir, if you will excuse me. If the heart is surrounded by parasympathetic vagus nerves, then it can be controlled on occasions—stopped, in fact. It's not uncanny, but a simple biological fact. The little Dogovers are products of an evolution which differs from ours."

"You talk unholy rubbish," said Essanits sternly. "Out of my way, if you please."

...

To WILL YOURSELF TO DEATH . . . The prisoner lay sprawled on the floor of a room, the dimensions of which he did not know. To will yourself to death. He strained every nerve, yet could not die. His heart functioned as part of his autonomic nervous system.

A sensation of burning numbness penetrated his entire body. He could think only of how good it would be to commit suicide simply by willpower, as the Dogovers did: their hearts must be, much like human breathing, part of a semiautonomic nervous system. Tolsteem had understood.

A bowl of soup was passed through the door flap. The prisoner's mouth was dry. He needed the liquid but could not order his limbs to move, to drag himself across the floor to the bowl.

Fading in and out of consciousness, he kept imagining he was drinking from the bowl. Then, rousing, he tasted only dust on a swollen tongue.

He swore to himself that in that other world he would not be a victim. That he swore, and swore again, even as they came and hauled him back for a further session of interrogation.

His interrogator this time was a small, weasel-faced man. Under a sharp little nose grew the bristles of a meager ginger mustache, much as a thistle grows in the shade of a rocky outcrop. His weak gray eyes were supplemented by a pair of metal-rimmed spectacles.

His opening statement, made in a thin voice, was not encouraging. "Many of your bastarding friends and conspirators have passed through our hands. Few are now alive. What precisely are your claims to be English?"

The prisoner said that his ID card gave his nationality as English.

"And your father's nationality?"

"He was born in Uganda. But I was born in England, in Ealing."

The little mustache twitched. "Your father was a black."

"No."

"Liar! Ugandans are black."

"We came from Hyderabad. We were not Ugandans, we are not blacks."

"What have you got against blacks?"

"We were immigrants."

"You're still a bastarding immigrant. You take advantage. You seek to undermine our culture. You lie, you cheat, you blow things up."

"Not me." A guard hit him in the stomach. He doubled up, gasping in pain.

"You blow things up, you shit! You're a fucking Muslim!"

"Please—*please*—let me explain . . ." He was gasping, hardly able to speak. "I do admire your culture, your freedom of speech as it used to be, and above all—"

"You liar! You published a book advocating the assassination of the prime minister."

Wearily, he wondered what had made this little man into the turd he was. He could hardly speak. He gasped that he had never advocated any such thing. Both guards began to beat him.

"You published a bastarding book about assassinating the prime minister. Do you deny that, you bastard?" Spit issued with the words. The voice was growing shriller.

"I do deny it. Please, please—it was just one silly sentence, a joke . . ."

The sharp little face darted forward. "You think that killing the PM is a bastarding joke? We'll show you what a bastarding joke is!"

Again the fists fell upon him, on his face, on other vulnerable areas. He was on the edge of a dark cliff. He fell over.

THE MATRIX OF SPACE was a howling wilderness of elementary particles. It was a fast-moving stew, a prototemporal storm of the lethally tiny. Light permeated it without time or direction: light simply was, in the darkness. This was where God would have lived—in a creative fury, spread like weed over a pond across the universe—had he existed.

For those with eyes that saw all over the electromagnetic spectrum, there would be beauty here. But for those who traveled on the great ship, far from their native habitat, merely as molecular components of the LPR, many things withered: not vocabulary alone.

The dreamself traveled through this chaos harmed, vindictive, destined for the alien planet.

THE INTERSTELLAR SHIP had been brought down—had crash-landed—outside what grew to be Stygia City, where it now stood as a memorial to the unique journey. Because there was more oxygen in the atmosphere than had been the case back on Earth, many parts of the ship were rusting. Nevertheless, work went on in the interior; this was the one place where workshops were set up and still functioning.

Fremant and the other guards accompanied Astaroth on a visit to the ship for one of his irregular inspections. On these occasions, Astaroth acted against his ascetic beliefs. He favored the scientists working here, and brought them a cartload of vegetables, of rydalls, hodgerks, jhamies, and the peppy dirdist, together with such fruits as busk and clammerdumm. Also meat: dacoims, jackrat, and portleg in particular.

The scientists were engaged in Operation Cereb, developing a mind-evaluator. The first phases of this complex scanning device had been researched during the final years of the ship's journey, in an effort to understand what precisely had gone wrong mentally with those who had lapsed into insanity. It was only here, in the bowels of the old ship, the *New Worlds*, that computers were allowed.

The project appeared to be going well, although never speedily enough for the great Astaroth. The scientists showed him, cringingly, the model-in-progress they had rigged up for the occasion.

After the inspection, a feast was held for the researchers on the M-E, along with their families and those who worked for them. A spirit of jollity prevailed. Astaroth, with Aster close at hand, and his Waabee clan stood to one side, looking on haughtily with barely disguised contempt for human weakness and the pleasures of the flesh.

A middle-aged man, a cleaner, came up with a plate of the golden busk and offered it with smiles to the leader.

"Go away," said Astaroth. "Give it to the peasants. I do not eat."

Sports were held. The highlight was billed as the Kontest. In a small rectangular arena two piles of small stones were arranged, no stone bigger than fifty millimeters in diameter. One pile was painted red, one blue. These were the weapons of the two contestants.

On this occasion, the contestants were both black, by name Chankey and Gragge. They fought naked to the death. Each might hurl stones only of their own designated color, blue or red. They might hurl the stones or punch each other. This was Kontesting.

And Fremant was the referee. His main duty was to see that Chankey and Gragge kept within the rectangle, and to announce when one contestant was truly dead.

Dunk! went the flung stones on flesh. *Dunk! Dunk!* The crowd cheered every stone that found its target. Gragge went down on one knee after a red struck his shin. Before he was up again, another red hit his shoulder. He was swift to recover. He flung a blue that missed and then a second that caught Chankey in the ribs. *Chunk!* Soon both men were reduced to crawling on the ground, both suffering serious injury. Snarling like wild beasts, they took ahold of each other. Each tried to throttle his opponent or to tear his throat out. Chankey managed to heave Gragge's upper body onto one of the stones. Grabbing another stone, a red, he began to bash his opponent's skull in. *Crack! Craaack!*

The audience cheered and laughed.

Gragge lay dead and broken, his brains spilling on the ground. Fremant waved his flag.

He helped Chankey to his feet. Blood poured down Chankey's torso. He collapsed, unconscious. A day or two later, Fremant happened to hear that Chankey had not died of his wounds and was making a slow recovery.

As Fremant left the field, Astaroth clapped him on his shoulder.

"You made a good showing, lad. I am keeping my eye on you!"

High praise, Fremant thought. Or was it a warning? He hated Astaroth for encouraging the brutal entertainment of the Kontest.

As ASTAROTH RODE OFF AHEAD in his chariot, Aster came up to Fremant. She pulled her hood aside, looking up at him from under her eyelashes. "I have decided to forgive you for what you did, you brute."

"Oh, why's that?" he asked coldly.

"Because I love you." She ceased to hold the hood in order to demonstrate with a flutter of hands how like a flame that love was. "Burning, burning love!"

He struggled with his emotions. Stygia City was so full of suspicion and secrets that he wondered if this woman might not be the one who would sink the Clandestine dagger into his heart.

"I'll buy you a glass of wine, Aster. Then we can talk it over."

She fell in beside him. He thought, as they walked, that wherever they went, people would see them. Word would get back to Astaroth. Better to take Aster to Bellamia's house; the old girl would not mind and could, he believed, be trusted to keep her mouth shut.

Dusk was coming on when he knocked at Bellamia's door. He was feeling resentful, yet wondering why he should be. The stout lady opened her door with caution, then stood back to let the two of them in.

"This is Aster, Bellamia," he said, as the girl drew aside her hood.

"I know who it is, right enough," the woman said, casting an ill look at Aster. He smelled salack on her breath.

They seated themselves at the table as Bellamia poured them each a glass of her buskade. The insect-parrot gave out its stridulous cry, unfolding a kind of watery score which faded as it unwound. Darkness was already gathering in the crowded little room; Fremant and Aster could scarcely see each other's faces across the table until Bellamia brought a lighted candle to set between them.

Aster stretched out her hand to Fremant. As he took it, he burst into complaint. "This backwater of a planet! No art forms here, no cinema, no discs, no personal computers. Not even paintings to hang on the walls."

Aster was defensive. "There were those pretty red and blue stones in the Kontest . . ."

"Not quite Picasso or Rembrandt, though, were they, eh?"

"Who were they?" Bellamia asked.

Could it be that he was the only person on this whole world who knew the name Rembrandt? Of course, all these people had been for countless years mere elements in the ship's LPR. He was a being apart. He could not think how he had come here. He had not been born on Stygia. He floundered in a morass of uncertainties, insecurities.

"But we don't need such things, dear," said Aster, ignoring Bellamia. "Life is better without them. Simpler! Art forms suggest too much, don't they? At least we live on a solid surface with the sky overhead. Isn't that enough?"

"No, it's not enough. We didn't create the sky overhead, did we?"

"But I thought art forms were responsible for—oh, I don't know what. People being—what do you call it? You know, stuck up on crosses, and like that."

"And music," said Bellamia, laughing. The room was heavy with the scent of her salack. "Was there music on Earth? It must be deliberate that we remember so little about that place." She turned and busied herself about her little stove.

"Art in general was once a major human concern," he said, scowling across at Aster in the candlelight. "Paintings, sculptures, books, music . . . back on Earth."

"Earth!" she said contemptuously. "That's long lost. Astaroth says we were all sent away for safety reasons. You have too much Earthblood in you. Are you forgetting how you were tortured there?"

"Oh, that!" he exclaimed, disconcerted. He had forgotten he had confided in Aster about the torture. A shadow crossed his psyche.

"Yes, *that*! You don't claim you have forgotten being tortured, do you? Oh, how you lie! I am surrounded—surrounded—by lies and deception. How can I bear it? I don't know . . ."

He shook his head. "Calm down, will you? The nightmares I was suffering—"

"You suffer nightmares! What do you think I suffer? Bringing me here to this low hovel—"

"What's the matter? Are you mad?"

She banged the palm of her hand on the table. "You were insane! Admit it!"

He stood up. "If you're going to insult me, why don't you just disappear—out of my life! You tricked me with the Clandestines, and I won't forget it."

With a quick movement Aster produced a knife. Baring her teeth, she pointed it at him. "What's so insulting about being insane in a mad world? If you attack me again, I swear I shall kill you this time!"

He seated himself, trying to out-stare her.

"You wouldn't dare."

"You raped me once and that's more than enough, you bluggerate."

"You can talk—it's certainly more than enough for me, let me tell you." He gripped the edge of the table, ready to overturn it if she made a move.

"Oh, I'd kill you gladly, gladly! What of your promise to kill Astaroth? Or have you forgotten that already, too?"

"I've not forgotten," he said sullenly.

"You've not acted."

Bellamia came up to the table, saucepan in hand. She *tut-tut*ted. "Now, stop this silliness. Love one another, damn you, if you must! But why all this quarreling? I'm getting you a nice stew of portleg tail to eat, so be quiet. Be quiet!"

"You be quiet," Aster told her, indignantly turning on her. "You're forgetting yourself. I am the mistress of the All-Powerful, so behave yourself."

With lowered brow, Bellamia said, "I know well enough who you are. And what you are."

The remark seemed to quell the younger woman. She put away her knife. Fremant sat down. They stared at each other, full of hatred and confusion. Then she stared down at the grain of the tabletop.

"This place stinks," Aster said quietly. "Why did you bring me here?"

Slowly their mood lightened and they began to behave more like friends, despite themselves, as if, in spite of everything, there was a bond between them. When the older woman served up her food, she, too, sat down at the table and ate with them. Aster made no protest. Nor did she complain about the food, flavored as it was with salack. The herb, at once bitter and sweet, was reputed to have a sedative effect on nerves.

"What did you do in your reconstituted years on the ship?" she asked Bellamia.

"Miss, when I was reconstituted out of the LPR, I was put in command of one shift of the laundry section. A hard job it was. Of course I was a younger woman then." Her eyes were half-closed, enfolded in flesh. "Much younger."

"Had you no man as partner?"

"He's long dead," said Bellamia, in a tone that defied further inquiry. She repeated, "Long dead . . ."

When Aster took her leave, she and Fremant kissed briefly outside the door. He took some breaths of fresh air before reentering the stuffy room.

BELLAMIA SAID TO FREMANT, "Mayhap I should not tell you this, but that young lady is the mistress of Astaroth, as she tells you. What she does not boast about is that she is his daughter as well."

"It can't be!" He was aghast.

With contempt, the old woman replied, "What you mean, 'It can't be'? You're soft in the head, my man. Many things as should not be *can* be. It's one of that kind I'm telling you about—one of that kind!"

DAWN, TWO DAYS LATER. High in the southern sky, casting pale shadows, sailed Stygia's six little broken moons, product of the cosmic collision of which the Shawl was also a result.

Fremant was on his way to report for duty at the Center. As he passed through the echoing empty squares, he began to suspect that someone was following him.

When he turned the next corner, he stopped there, shoulders to the wall, waiting. Sure enough, in a moment, another man turned the corner, a tall, thin man with a stoop. Fremant struck him hard on the side of his skull with his right fist. The man's jaw fell open. He sank to his knees and collapsed.

Fremant dragged the man into a side alley and sat astride him.

"Okay, you funker, whose side are you on?"

The man muttered something incomprehensible.

"Speak clearly or I'll poke your eyes out. Who are you?"

"Name's Webshider. Let me up, dammit!"

"Who's paying you to tail me?" As he was asking, he was searching in Webshider's pockets. He found some stigs and pocketed them. From an inner concealment he fished out a bone-handled knife with a curved blade. He flung it far down the alley.

"Come on, who's paying you?"

"No one. It's voluntary. Let me up. Please."

"You were going to kill me, you scum! For the last time, who are you working for?" He shook the man's throat until his skull rattled against the paving stone.

"The Clandestines. The Clandestines, all right?"

Fremant smacked him across the chops. "Those useless wretches? Look, if I spare your life, you'll go slinking back to them and their nameless god. Tell them from me they are crap. Tell them they should mingle with the ordinary population to foment discontent, get it? Not just hide out across the lake, get it? Foment discontent, get people to understand they can demonstrate in force, get it? One big demonstration and we can kick Astaroth out, get it?"

Each "get it?" was accompanied by a fist in Webshider's ribs.

"You'll never manage to kick Astaroth out, you bully," the man gasped.

"Try it!"

"You'll never manage it because the people here are—I dunno—sort of sick after the long journey and Reconstitution."

He propped the thin man up and rested his back against the wall. "You're saying there was something the matter with the LPR, the Life Process Reservoir?"

"How do I know?" the other responded. "It's possible, ain't it? Or else this planet don't agree with us. Maybe there's some sort of germ in the air that—"

"You scum! You're sick." He gave the shuddering face another slap.

"We're all sick, you bluggerate—because we are dumped here to live among aliens and insects."

The notion struck a chord in Fremant's mind. "It's a rule of life—we all have to live among strangers . . . Get yourself back to that Habander feller and tell him what I've said, okay?"

He stood up and watched alertly as Webshider struggled slowly to his feet, gasping and groaning. He was not a fighting man. Fremant gave him a kick in his rear as he slouched off.

He then hurried in the direction of the Center, afraid of reporting in late.

THREE

THE ROSY-FACED STABLE MAID, Breeth, made Fremant and Tunderkin bowls of sweet otz, which she cooked over a little fire in the tack room. After that, they brought out the horses and brushed them down under the pale sky. High above their heads rode one of the six moons.

"How do you call that moon?" Fremant asked. His mood was still bad from the fight in the alley, and his knuckles hurt.

"Why, 'tis Brother, of course," said Breeth with a smile. "How come you don't know that?"

"So you know the names of all the moons?"

"Indeed I do, as do everyone, 'cos they're all named the same." She laughed. "It's Brother the lot of them, ain't it?"

"But they're all different."

"No, you silly, they're all moons."

Pulling Hengriss from the stable to make the beast piss in the yard, Tunderkin said, "Got to be extra care with this one. This one is Essanits's steed."

"What difference does that make?" Fremant asked.

"My old gran knew the types of folks she met with. You, Fremant, you're always asking questions, you'd be the Eternal Stranger."

He thought the observation was acute. He was eternally a stranger, even to himself.

"And how would your old gran typecast Astaroth?"

"Mad stallion . . ."

They began to brush down the horses. The animals stood still, their sides heaving in and out as they breathed through them, unaware their lives were passing, unaware even that they were alive in the full sense of the word.

"You ask too many questions. You'll get in trouble." Tunderkin ducked his head below the flank of Hengriss, to say in a low tone, "My old gran was one who saw into men's minds. She'd say them as are tortured are the torturers. Now, shut your face and let's get these beasts saddled up for morning inspection."

The day was still chilly and the breath of the horses hung about them as they tacked up the patient beasts.

DAYS WORE BY and once more the Shawl covered the sky, darkening Stygia City, cooling the planet. Astaroth retreated into his private quarters, taking Aster with him. The so-called World Council, nominally under WAA supervision, was left in charge. Headless, it did nothing. Only Essanits was prepared to make decisions.

Although the appearance of the Shawl in its orbit was completely predictable, appearing over Stygia City as it did every ten days, the populace, according to its own slow-moving destiny, was so wrapped in inertia that no one ever made preparations for its arrival. A number of people died on every occasion that the Shawl passed overhead.

It was Essanits who set up a store where a slender ration of food could be obtained by any who needed it. Those who claimed food in this way had their forefinger dipped in a purple dye so that they could not make a repeat visit. This forethought on Essanits's part saved many malnourished lives.

On the second day after its appearance overhead, the Shawl sank toward the western horizon. Normal life was resumed. A day later, Astaroth came roaring from his den, all boots and flowing robes. The food store was being shuttered when Astaroth came on it. Fremant and Cavertal, another guard, had to accompany him. Astaroth raged at the wastage. Yet he said not a word of reproof to Essanits, such was the aura of immunity which seemed to envelop the younger man.

Instead, Astaroth attacked one of Essanits's stallholders.

"Why give away food? Men must earn their living, their very bread. That is a basic law of life."

"Without food they might have died, sir, and had no law." The man hung his head, in fear at any attempt to contradict the leader.

"Then they should have died. Those who would die are the ones who have no sense, who would not store food."

Essanits, standing by, arms akimbo, said mildly, "Some of the poor are unable to afford to buy anything ahead of time, sir. They have to live from hand to mouth, if I may remind you."

"You may, Soldier Essanits," replied Astaroth, controlling his anger, "and I will remind you that such men are worth nothing to our community. The days of the egalitarian society we had on the ship after LPR in its final years are long over. Here we must fight for our living."

Fremant could not resist speaking out. "Then those who have been saved from starvation are now able to fight for that living. Our community is too small for us not to value every single body on Stygia."

Astaroth turned to survey his guard. "Our need is for real men, not for weaklings or impertinent dogs like you. Guard"— he pointed at Cavertal—"arrest this man! Relieve him of his weapons at once. Three days in the cells."

"That's unjust! I merely wished to point out—"

"Silence! You do wrong to speak at all!"

Essanits said, "He did no harm, sir. What he said is true. We are underpopulated. Would you arrest a man for speaking truth?" He stood rigidly upright, handsome, grim, prepared to confront the All-Powerful.

"A guard must hold his tongue in my presence." Astaroth drew himself up as if he were a guard himself. Then he looked away with a dismissive shake of his head.

Cavertal reluctantly did as he was bid. With a length of leather, he lashed Fremant's hands behind his back and marched him off.

Beneath the Center were cellars and prison cells. In no time, Fremant found himself thrust into one such cell.

"Sorry, pal," said Cavertal in a low voice. "But you was asking for trouble, crossing him like that." He slammed the door on his friend.

Astaroth, meanwhile, retired to his quarters, still vexed that he had been contradicted. Aster had retired to her room, saying she was unwell. Astaroth fumed but did nothing. Instead, he put his booted feet up on a chair and summoned his old wife, Ameethira, to keep him company.

"It's funny," she said, "but I keep getting headaches. I take a walk every day, except when the Shawl is overhead, of course, but still I have a headache."

Speaking mildly but in his usual tone of contempt, he told her she was always complaining.

Paper-white, she asked in a quiet voice, "Do you wish to know where I walk?"

"Why should I care where you walk?" He glared at her shriveled form with contempt, at her old, torn clothes, which seemed to mark her out as a prisoner.

"I walk to the edge of the cliffs and I stand there and stare at the sea. It never rests. The waves never cease. And what do you imagine I think about?"

"How should I know what you think about, woman?"

"I think about throwing myself off the cliffs into the sea. That's what I think about."

She gave a sort of laugh and peered shortsightedly at her husband to judge his response.

"Go away," he said. "Get out of my sight!"

She seemed to weaken. She held out a supplicatory hand. "Do you ever recall, Astaroth, the days when I was first reconstituted and was young and beautiful and you loved me?"

"Those days are gone," he said, and scowled down at the floor. "No personal relationships anymore . . ."

After some while, when she felt like it, Aster appeared. "Mother Ameethira is not happy," she said.

"What do you expect?" He told Aster to fetch him a glass of buskade.

"That young big mouth, Fremant—I am tired of his voice, tired of his face. He's rotting in the cells at present. I'll get rid of the little snot."

"Fremant?" She was startled to hear his name. "Why, he's a good guardsman, isn't he? Punctual, loyal . . ."

"What do you know about it?" he asked.

"I happen to like him, that's all." She looked nervous. Her hands twisted about ceaselessly.

He grasped the arms of his chair. His face went red. His eyes bulged. "I had a report . . . Fool I was to ignore it. That you were seen with some young fellow. It was Fremant, wasn't it? You dare slip away from me into his arms?'

"No, no, Papa! It wasn't he! Honestly—"

Astaroth bounded up and seized her by the wrist. He dragged her to his chair, forcing her to kneel abjectly before him.

"Now, then—you've been doing it with that little snot, haven't you? I could smell it on you!"

"Oh no, please—"

He struck her across the face with an open palm. "You did, didn't you, you little whore? Admit it, or I'll strangle you here and now!"

She screamed. He struck her again. Her lip was bleeding. Tears burst from her eyes at the pain.

"Oh no, no, please, Papa, please! You hurt me so!"

Astaroth thrust his burning face into hers. "I'll hurt you more unless you tell me the truth. What did you do with him?" He grasped her throat and squeezed.

Aster gave a faint cry. She opened her mouth to gasp for air.

"He raped me . . . Just as you did!" The words were gasped out. "Let me go, you brute!"

He let her go, let her crumple to the floor, sobbing, sobbing at both her pain and her confession, knowing what it entailed.

FREMANT WAS LYING ON THE FLOOR of his cell, half-alive. The leader had burst into his cell and set about him with a cudgel, beating him here, beating him there. He felt as if every bone in his body were broken.

"You'll stay here till I kill you," said Astaroth, out of breath. "I'll be back to deal with you again tomorrow."

So, very well, then. It was to be death. He had but one day more to breathe, to exist, to sprawl on the cold stone.

Astaroth, like many lesser men, believed in revenge.

Fremant had heard that there was a religion somewhere which believed not in revenge but in its opposite, forgiveness.

Forgiveness . . . the very word had a gentle touch, whereas *revenge* was like a sword dragged over cold stone. And yet forgiveness was so much harder to grant.

What had been said? He could hardly think, but in spasms it came to him. Yes, "turning the other cheek" . . . That had been a tenet of a great religion, a religion now lost.

In how many countries, how many tribes, were vendettas an abiding source of misery because it was held to be honorable never to forgive . . .

Well, that meant nothing now, if tomorrow marked the end of all things, all hopes, all mistakes . . .

. . .

"I'll die," he whispered to himself. "I'll die. For sure I'll die." He saw above him a grille of iron bars which served to let in a glimmer of light.

The darkness whirled about him, the sight of light was lost.

"You'll not die until you have answered our questions," said another voice. "Doris was your wife. Where were you married? In some fucking mosque?"

"In a registry office in Harrow . . . I shall surely die . . ."

"Tell me her name."

"I told you more than once. Doris."

"Doris *who*, you bastard?"

"Doris McGinty." He felt he would crumble from fatigue. They had kept him awake for fifty hours without rest.

"She was a white woman."

"She was Irish."

"She was a white woman, you bastard."

"Yes."

"How did you manage to marry a white woman?"

"Oh, for God's sake. I thought this was a free country."

"So it was, until you bastards started blowing things up, uttering threats, suicide-bombing."

"That was nothing to do with me. I was a lawful law-abiding citizen."

"But you were thinking of blowing the place up. You were an ally of this shit from Al-Muhajiroun. You wrote about killing the PM in your sodding book."

"That was just a—just a joke, really . . . A bit unfortunate . . ."

The guard struck him across the nape of his neck with a wooden baton. He heard the small bones crunch.

A deep bespattered darkness fell upon him.

...

ESSANITS CAME TO VISIT HIM IN HIS CELL.

"I find you in a bad way, Fremant," he said. "I'm permitted to be in these cellars because our leader regards me as a hero. Because . . ." Here his voice faltered. "Because I wiped out the Dogovers."

Fremant could not raise his voice above a whisper. "He will kill me tomorrow. I know that."

"Astaroth's reign of injustice must end, and with it his hateful creed. You have spirit. I cannot let you die. It's against my"—he pronounced a word Fremant vaguely understood—"religion."

About his neck Essanits wore a length of scarf. This he removed and went over to the iron bars of the grille. Standing on tiptoe, he tied the scarf to one of the bars.

"When it is dark, I shall return outside the Center. The scarf will tell me which is your cell. I will give you further instructions then. Meanwhile . . ."

He brought from his pocket a quantity of salack. "Chew this. Rest yourself. Fear nothing."

Essanits left.

Fremant propped himself against a wall and chewed on the herb. Gradually, some of his strength returned.

The day waned. A jailer came, bringing a small pitcher of water and a hunk of bread. The bread tasted stale. Fremant washed it down with gulps of water.

As darkness closed in, Fremant detected—so sensitized was he by now to such things—an additional alteration in the light; he realized that the Shawl was about to pass over Stygia once again.

When darkness became complete, and a chilly wind blew through his grating, he heard a sound outside. The scarf was removed from the bars. A glowworm of light showed. Then came a dull clumping of a heavy instrument striking the mortar in which the bars were embedded. A pause. The bars were being tested, shaken. More clumping. A bar was being wrenched away. Then another bar. Then another.

A hand extended into the prison cell, holding a small light in a glass. It was followed by a rope. The light was the signal. It was withdrawn.

Fremant grasped the rope, tested it to see that it was secure, then seized it firmly and climbed up the wall. He wriggled his way through the toothless gap of his window, to arrive on all fours on the ground outside. Willing hands helped him to his feet. Someone clapped him on his back.

"Horses nearby," said Essanits. "Are you all right? Let's hurry!"

They guided him downhill, a young unknown man holding tightly to the escaped prisoner's arm to prevent him falling. It was the darkest of nights. No one was about. Not a glimmer of light showed in any window. There was no doubt that the passing of the Shawl awoke superstitious dread in local hearts, and not in Astaroth's alone.

They hurried into a side street heading away from the Center. Cats scurried off at their approach. Four men were accompanying Fremant—Essanits and three younger men.

"Steady!" Essanits ordered. They slowed their pace.

A thickset man was waiting for them in the street ahead. He emerged from a doorway, where he had been lounging against the doorpost, to beckon them in. They were led along a narrow passageway and through another door, where the air was heavy with the smell of hay and horses and the noise of clawed hooves restless on tile.

This stranger shook Fremant's hand with his leathery one. "I'm the stablekeeper," he said in a deep voice. "I help Essanits against my better judgment, see?"

Fremant could barely speak in reply.

A lantern hung from a beam in the stable. Fremant was able to see his rescuers. Essanits he recognized immediately—the tall, well-shaped man with a large, square, clean-shaven face and deep-set eyes. His mouth, with its pale lips, seemed to spread across his face. The younger men in his company looked much alike, all stressed and anxious, differing most clearly in hairstyles: One had plentiful locks, one had fair hair cut almost to stubble, and the third was prematurely bald.

"All right," said Essanits, "we're going to make for the hills. I know a place where you'll be safe, a little township called Haven. Some religion prevails there. The sooner we leave here, the better."

Under the stablekeeper's supervision, certain of the best horses were in the process of being saddled.

These insects bore little resemblance to ordinary horses. However, they were sturdy creatures, with pronounced hind legs, and fully capable of carrying a human burden. They had been bred for strength. Since their lives were comparatively short, breeding had rapidly taken place. They had been bred for distinctive colors as well as strength. Fremant couldn't help viewing them with suspicion.

The beasts fought against saddling, as if well aware of the cold outside and the hardship to come. Kicking and rearing, they managed to fill the air with fragments of straw; so much so that one of Essanits's youths, the frailest one, by name Hazelmarr, went into a sneezing fit.

Recovering slightly, he spoke pleadingly, "Essanits, sir, I'm not up to this adventure, I fear. You must do without me, as I am sure you can well manage."

Essanits stared hard at him, while the other two young men tried to argue Hazelmarr out of his decision. "Very well," said Essanits. "If you have no faith or stomach, then go. Speak to no one of this, you understand?"

Hazelmarr nodded dumbly, shaking his head of hair, but as he turned to leave, the stablekeeper grabbed him by the arm. "You can't let this little snot go, just like that," he told Essanits. "He'll tell on you for sure. I know his kind—you can't trust 'em. A real snake, he is!"

"So you plan to kill him?" said Essanits coldly.

"That's the way to make sure he stays silent, ain't it?"

"Let him go, man, will you? He may be a coward, but he doesn't deserve to die."

With that, Hazelmarr was allowed to sneak away into the night, assisted by the stablekeeper's boot.

Fremant, Essanits, and the two remaining youths mounted their selected horses. Fremant was on a skewbald called Snowflake. Its vestigial wings creaked as he settled himself in the saddle.

After Essanits had given the stablekeeper a bag of stigs, they made their way out to the street in single file.

"I must stop by to pay Bellamia," Fremant told Essanits. "I owe her for my room."

"Forget about that," said the fair-haired Oniversin. "We need to get out of town fast."

Essanits reined his horse. "Fremant is good and honest. All men should pay their debts. To Bellamia's house, then. It will take but a minute extra."

Bellamia was asleep. It took a good deal of hammering at her door to rouse her. She opened the door only a crack, to show them she had a cudgel in her hand, and to swear at them.

"You've already got me into trouble, you devil," she told Fremant, who had dismounted. "Some brutes from the Center was round here asking all about you. Said I should not have lodged you. I'm in fear of my life, I am."

"Look, Bellamia, we're in great haste. Here's the money I owe you."

He held the money out to her.

"Money's no good to me if my throat's cut, is it now?" She pulled her door wide open. "Here, take me with you, wherever you're going. I'll cook for the lot of you."

"It means trouble to take a woman with us," said Ragundy, the bald youth.

"I'll give you trouble if you trouble me," she told him.

Bellamia had been sleeping in her clothes and now appeared ready to leave immediately.

"What about the parrot?" Fremant asked.

"To hell with the parrot," she replied. "I'll let it go free."

After a short argument, Essanits ordered her to mount his horse behind him and to hold tight. He hauled her into position. Then they were off.

THE CONTINENT ON THE EDGE of which Stygia City perched had long ago tipped toward the ocean. Thus, leaving Stygia City to travel inland entailed a steady climb upward—not exactly steep at first, but unremitting: unremitting until the horsemen came, on the second day, to a veritable hill, which marked the beginning of more broken terrain, and a different kind of land.

"Everyone dismount," Essanits ordered. He helped Bellamia down from his horse.

The others also dismounted, looking about them rather uncertainly.

"We must offer thanks to God for keeping us in safety so far."

"God?" exclaimed Ragundy. "We left God behind long since."

"Jesus Christ visited this planet only for a short while, leaving never to return. From that absence stem many of our problems," Essanits declared. He lifted his eyes. "We offer thanks to God, if he is listening, for our safety so far, and for our arrival in a territory where we are free of the pollutions of Stygia City. Keep us steadfast and may we enter more fully into your mind. Amen."

Embarrassed, Fremant and Ragundy muttered their own amens in response.

Ragundy asked if God's mind included women. To which Essanits replied patiently, "You will always try to vex me, Ragundy. You voice your own troubled character. When you tire of doing so, you will move nearer to God and feel happier. I pray for that day."

Bellamia was more strident. "Just supposing there was a god, he'd be more likely to include me than a little dottle like you!"

"Ah, shut up, the pair of you," said Oniversin.

"We must all hold our tongues," said Essanits, "in the hope that good sense may thereby govern our lips."

Fremant asked what they were going to do now.

Wordlessly, Essanits flung up an arm and pointed into the hills.

They mounted their horses, which had been grazing, and headed onward again.

Now there was a faint trail, leading among boulders. Some boulders were the size of houses. Many had streaks of colored clay in them, yellow zigzags through the rock. At the feet of these boulders grew various plants. Some were in bloom, bearing modest black-and-white petals. Bellamia wanted to dismount to pick some but Essanits would not stop.

As the horses picked their way along, small wingless birdlike insects flitted among the boulders, clucking their disgust at human intrusion.

On the following day, they came on a more open space, where the ground was level. Ahead of them lay a small hill. On the hill, and below it, stood a scatter of houses.

"Yonder is Haven," said Essanits, "where we shall be favorably received."

It was as he said. Nearer the houses, they dismounted so as not to appear formidable to a small group of people who were coming to greet them.

The greetings were serious and unsmiling but friendly nevertheless. The newcomers were welcomed into the village, Fremant leading Snowflake. He felt the strangeness of the place; the sense of being an Eternal Stranger, as Breeth had called him, came upon him. He struggled with himself.

"Thanks be to Jesus Christ, who guided us here," Essanits had said to the crowd, before dismounting.

Many of the cottages were built on stilts, with ladders leading up to the living quarters. Insectoid creatures resembling small goats were kept tethered under the houses, together with an occasional horse, and the roofs of the houses were covered with turf. A forge and a stable with horses for hire stood together on one side of the square. Another house sold milk and cheese of a kind called katchkall.

A stiltless cottage housed a potter; behind his cottage was a litter of broken pots, their brown fragments resembling the wreckage of the shells of marine creatures. Above the potter, Fremant was told, lived a man, a hermit, who made clothes. One of the houses standing on what served as the village square was reserved for guests, and here the newcomers were installed.

On the whole, the village of Haven did not present a welcoming appearance. Centuries of technology had brought these humans here; now they gave every appearance of having sunk back to Earth's Middle Ages.

It seemed to Fremant at first that the population of Haven consisted either of babies or of the aged. Instead of sounds of music came the sound of babies crying, or at the least uttering cries. He found the cries particularly unnerving. On closer inspection, the aged were less aged than withered, worn out by their labors in the fields. The seed stored in the holds of the *New Worlds*, which had brought them to Stygia, was unsuited to the soil of Stygia. And the soil was mainly barren, as many readily complained.

Despite its name, Haven was a harsh environment, where music and laughter were lacking. An old man, by name Deselden, reinforced the gloom with his sermons—to which most people listened, for want of better entertainment.

Essanits was known here and given a courteous welcome. In

particular, two rows of neatly dressed children, one of boys, one of girls, sang a chant for their visitor, repeating over and over the phrase, "May you find some comfort here, and in Jesus." After their song, they stood quietly, well-behaved under the control of a gray-haired woman who introduced herself as Liddley. She was known as "The Schoolteacher."

The portly elder by the name of Deselden, who clearly wielded local authority, gave a rambling speech and uttered a prayer, long in words and strong in self-abasement, in Essanits's honor, to which Essanits responded in kind. That evening, they were served a frugal meal, on the understanding that they would have to cook for themselves the next day. Bellamia was pleased to hear that.

"The water from their well tastes vile," she said, behind her hand. "Vile! I'll have to boil every drop of it or else we'll fall ill."

The horses were stabled below the guest house. When the company lay on mattresses to sleep, the restless movements of the horses could be heard beneath their heads.

The noise sounded like doors slamming. As Fremant lay drowsing, the cries came to him again, and he could hear men talking.

One voice was familiar. He remembered the cultivated American tones from long ago. The name came back to him on a tide of fear. Abraham Ramson! With the recognition dawned the knowledge that he was lying shackled on a hard floor.

Abraham Ramson was saying, ". . . wasting our time. Set him free, Algy. He's a nobody. He wants to feel British. He has some English or Irish wife, whatever her name is, and he has written what he thinks is a funny book. I scanned it. It's stupid and harmless."

Another voice said, "But he does talk about the prime minister being assassinated."

Ramson replied. "So what? I am inclined to believe him when he says it was intended as humor. Had he really planned to assassinate your PM, he would hardly be likely to put the idea into print, would he, now?"

"Okay, so what? You advocate setting him free, Abraham?"

"Sure do. Show the little bastard mercy. Kick him out on the street! Get rid of him! He's free to go."

"ENJOY WHAT YOU CALL YOUR FREEDOM," Essanits told Fremant. "You can live here in Haven and regain spiritual qualities." He and Fremant, together with Bellamia, Ragundy, and Oniversin, were breaking their fast with bread and honey and glasses of water from the village well. The water did indeed taste vile.

After the meal, Fremant and Ragundy took a walk about the village. Fremant tried to shake off the hollow feeling that he was not really here. "I must be sick," he told himself. A large cross stood on one side of the square, to which Ragundy drew their attention. "That's Essanits's sign," he said. "You must know by now he's a bit cracked about this feller Jesus. Who was Jesus, do you know? I don't remember him from the ship."

"So much has been lost."

"But do we want it back? Present's bad enough without Jesus."

"He was assassinated, that's all I know, or care." He sighed, thinking of his vow to kill Astaroth.

They had reason to learn more that evening. Haven was quiet during the day. Late in the afternoon, the villagers returned wearily from the fields, some bringing livestock with them. Their faces were worn. Many went straight to lie down awhile. They congregated in the square as the sun was setting behind the shoulder of a distant mountain, and Elder Deselden addressed them.

" 'Why did we come this long way from our home planet?' That is a question often on our lips, the big question we often ask ourselves. 'Why did we come this long way?' Is it not like the case of old age, when we see we have come a long way from our childhood? We have with us visitors who have come just a short way, from Stygia City. But Stygia City is a long way distant where the spirit is concerned. There in that city, the laws of wicked men, Astaroth and his party, rule. Here in Haven, we submit to the rule of none other than Jesus Christ.

"At the least, we *try* to submit to Christ's rule, because his rule is spiritual freedom, and spiritual freedom is hard to win. We must always strive for it, as best we can.

"There is honor in being poor, not least because Christ Jesus was poor. Christ never came to this world. He never set foot on Stygia. We eke out our existence on unhallowed ground. For that very reason God looks down on us all with contempt, and we must humble ourselves. If we do so, sincerely, with all our hearts, we shall in the end be with Christ to live in a glory very different from how we live now.

"Brother Essanits, the great saint of our order, will pray for our salvation."

At these words, all present bowed their heads, or all but Ragundy, who whispered to Fremant, "No offense, but I'm off . . ." He disappeared.

Essanits said in a loud voice, "Lord God, I do not believe, as our brother, Deselden, does, that you look down upon us in contempt, nor even with loving judgment. I do not believe you look upon us at all, having decided that we have all sinned by killing off the native people of Stygia, the Dogovers. In that, I am the most guilty. I was a slave to the will of the people, and of Astaroth. When I saw all those dead bodies, for which I must bear responsibility, I cried—and then, O God, then you saw my tears.

"I believe that Jesus walked on this planet, looking for us, and did not find us.

"Cast your eyes upon us, Lord God, and bless us and this planet we have inherited, so that we may live in peace with ourselves, and not in eternal torment. Amen."

"Amen," said the crowd, uplifted. They then looked about themselves as if coming out of a daze. A woman with a small child clutched to her breast knelt and kissed Essanits's hand, but most people appeared not to know what to do next, drifting off to their various cottages.

Elder Deselden took Essanits aside. Four disciples came with him, humble and anxious. Deselden spoke controlledly, but his look was one of hate. "Brother, you contradict my teachings and you speak heresy. Jesus never walked here. This is a heathen place, filled with alien life without a god. You blaspheme to say that Jesus ever set foot here. You think insects have a god? I forbid you to address my people again."

Essanits controlled his anger; but later he said to the grayhaired woman, Liddley, who attended him, that he understood Elder Deselden to lay claim of ownership to much of the land thereabouts, which was an unholy thing to do.

Liddley said in response, "Land should be free, as air and

water are free. But the land is overrun by little dacoims, which spoil the crops. By promising to rid us of dacoims, so Master Deselden took control of the land. Still the dacoims come and multiply, so Deselden keeps a hold on the land."

Having listened carefully, Essanits was puzzled. "How is that?" he asked.

The woman looked around her nervously. "Once a year he holds a shooting party, to kill the dacoims by the dozen. Only he can afford the guns and the bullets."

He frowned at her. "Where does he get guns and bullets from?"

She gestured helplessly. "They're made locally. A gunsmith by name Utrersin. A good man in a bad trade."

"But how does this holy man afford such things?"

She sighed heavily. "We who work on the land pay Deselden a small tithe of our earnings. It's little enough, but it keeps most of us in poverty."

He laid his hands on her head and looked with sorrow into her gray eyes. He blessed her.

As a result of Essanits's display of holiness, Fremant was afraid to speak to him. He sought out the company of Bellamia, and her usual good sense.

Bellamia was up to her elbows in flour in a large bowl. "This flour, such as it is, I can turn into a crust for a pie. It will be quite diff'rent. I can't see how Essanits can turn folk into something quite diff'rent. If God had wanted us to be decent people, he could have made us decent. Why not?"

"We do try to be decent, Bellamia."

"Some do, some don't. But why make it so hard? So damned

hard . . . The whole setup of life is against us. You have to grab what you can get, don't you? I mean, to survive. Just to survive."

Fremant did not agree. The long journey from Earth had been made in the hope of finding a better place. It was just a pity that various factions had sprung up on the ship after Reconstitution. But you could claim, he said, that life was better, if harder, in Haven than in the city they had left.

"No, that ain't so. We were sheltered in Stygia City. These folk here live like beasts, scraping a living from the land, and they've got this cult thing to plague them. Who's this Jesus they're on about, I'd like to know?"

"Well, the children appear happy and content, on the whole."

"Appear? *Appear?* All sorts of things *appear*, don't they, dear?"

Privately, Fremant thought to himself that Bellamia's mind was not likely to open up to new ideas. He saw that Essanits was a tormented man, and that the idea of a benevolent god looking down from space was calming to his spirit. For the present, his thoughts went no further than that.

He awoke on the following morning to the realization he was free. There was nothing he had to do, no questions he had to answer, no duties to perform for a harsh master. He found it an uneasy sensation, as if he had suddenly ceased to have a function. He asked himself if he should not be unrestrainedly glad to be free. Yet there was a shadow behind his thought.

He ventured to say as much, rather jokingly, to Essanits, over breakfast.

"Only in the service of God are we truly free."

Essanits's statement irritated Fremant.

"That's not what I mean by free."

Essanits looked at him with a half-smile on his broad face.

"Doubtless. What you mean by 'free' is to be at the mercy of your own random desires. What *I* mean by being free is free to travel down a straight road toward the perfect life of Christ."

He thought Essanits was mad. Essanits smiled and nodded, well in agreement with himself.

"How can you know about this 'perfect life of Christ'?"

"Happily, certain important discs survived the havoc of those final years on the ship."

Fremant looked for Bellamia but she was nowhere to be seen. He inquired of Liddley, who said she had seen her going to work with a local man who made clothes.

"It's none of your business what she does," said Liddley, with a smile.

Fremant eyed her challengingly. "You have a certain air of independence about you. How's that?"

Liddley made a dismissive gesture. "I have escaped from the land. My man works there but I have little in common with him. He does not think. I earn a pittance looking after people and children. That forces you to think . . ."

She pulled aside a sort of cape which covered her torso, to reveal a small child cradled there.

Fremant stared at it aghast. It was yellow of flesh. Its little arms were showing, clutching the cloth which supported it; they were thin as chicken legs. It did not move.

"This is the way I get my living," said Liddley. "Apart from my teaching work, for which parents pay me what little they can."

The mite at her breast had an overlarge hairless skull. Its body was withered, seemingly age-old. It stared unblinkingly at Fremant with opaque eyes, mouth drawn into a smile of queer meditative mirth.

"What is it?" he asked.

"She's dying," said Liddley, without emotion. She restored the cape over the baby. "Stygia doesn't suit her. Sleep now, poor little love . . ."

FREMANT WAS TIRED OF SORROW and of sorrowing people. He needed something—he knew not what. At least he could be free to enjoy a little solitude.

He roamed out on the nearby hillsides, enjoying the fresh air, the songs of the various insects, the color and life of everything in his view. Sometimes he lay on the small, brittle herbs that grew here, stretched out, staring into the sky, gazing into its depths as into the depths of a clear pool.

Dacoims were abundant. He watched them. They were frisky little things, armor-plated, with large baby eyes—presumably, he guessed, so that they could see during Dimoff.

For many days he walked, entranced by what he thought of as the emptiness of the country. He came to a small pool, fed by a stream and shaded by an old tree. The sweet sound of flowing water detained him. He stripped off his few clothes, to search his body for signs of torture, the scars that tyranny had left, like markings on a map. He found nothing. Since he was naked, he plunged into the pool. The cold of the water made him gasp.

He struck out vigorously, kicking the water into a foam with his legs and feet.

Something else was swimming there. It came up from the depths at him, curious, or perhaps hungry. In sudden alarm, he grasped it and flung it onto the bank. It lay thrashing. He climbed out after it.

The creature was two feet long, clad in chitin scales which the water had smoothed against its body. It was certainly not a fish, having no fins or gills. There were four clawlike appendages, which reached up to grasp Fremant. The head, attached to an ungainly body, appeared only slightly similar to a human's, while its protruding jaws suggested something like a bird's beak. He stood over it. It stared up at him with four multifaceted eyes, making low continuous noises.

He shivered to look at it, was frightened of it; taking up a stone, he smashed its skull, which delivered forth a foaming, creamy mass. Then he regretted doing so. Had the creature been hostile? he asked himself. Perhaps it had been merely curious, as he was curious.

He knelt by it to examine it and its sexual quarters. The longing for a woman came upon him—for a woman's embrace, for her ardor and pleasure; for her love.

He remained, thinking, on the bank, the sound of the water unheeded. Here was this miraculous world of Stygia, almost unexplored, little understood. Why did men not explore it, instead of dividing into factions and quarreling, one group against another group? Did they fear it so much? Maybe if they ventured into the interior they would find this Jesus walking there, robed in purity.

At length he stood up. He gazed into the water, wondering if the dead creature had a mate lurking in its depths. He did not venture into the pool again.

After days of wandering, he came to a small valley where salack grew profusely, low to the ground. It flowered with a little blue-and-white flower, very sweet smelling. He gathered handfuls of it and made himself a bed. The scent had a dizzying effect, not unpleasant. He made no attempt to eat it.

As he was lying there, a flying creature, with wings that might have been cut from colored paper, and a long stalklike tail, settled on his chest. Alarmed, Fremant, in one quick movement, seized it in his fist and crushed it to death. He sat up in fear and revulsion, shaking its sappy remains from his hand. He was in an alien land. He did not know whether or not such insects were harmless.

And he thought of himself, Always this impulse to kill . . .

Nor did he know what beasts might roam the country, which consisted of savannah, scrub, and small trees. In the region where he now found himself, small twittering things like grasshoppers, walking on long legs, often came near him in the daytime. They scampered off when he tried to approach. In the day, they seemed playful; but as the sun set and dusk drew on, these creatures sought refuge in the branches of small trees, weaving webs for cradles, to become silent and huddle together, clutching one another.

Fremant inferred from this that there must be large predators on the prowl by night. He also took to a safe tree, driving off the grasshopper-things in order to have the upper branches to himself. It was chillier there than on the ground but, he was sure, safer. He, too, wished he had someone to huddle with. He slept badly, unsure of what might lurk below, at ground level.

Sometimes he seemed to be freezing, sometimes floating.

Rousing one night, he saw the Brothers trailing overhead. They shed a fugitive light on the world below. He watched them with a sort of longing. In the LPR for centuries of space travel, the mortals preserved there had lost all personal characteristics, all history of personal relationships. Men had no wives, women no mothers. Only overhead remained the symbolic relationship of brotherhood. The future was everyone's dubious bride.

In his exhaustion, as he turned restlessly, he thought he heard the tread of predators. All was confusion. Was it two—or was it three—days since they had allowed him to sleep? He was made to stand in a corridor by a closed door. A guard watched over him. He was weak. He had stood there shivering for an hour, two hours. He fought against the tears of weakness that threatened.

Although he longed not to be standing there, he feared what would be his treatment when they summoned him into the room.

They summoned him in.

It was a small, windowless room. It contained only a bare table and two chairs. One of the chairs was an armchair. He stared at it longingly, not daring to approach it.

A casually dressed man with an open-neck shirt entered the room by a rear door.

He gestured toward the armchair.

"Do, please, sit down. I must apologize for keeping you waiting." He turned smilingly to the guard. "You can leave us now, Charlie. We'll get on fine on our own, thanks."

By way of introduction, he said that the prisoner could call him "Dick."

He was clean-shaven and in his mid-forties, of good complexion. His dark hair was long and rumpled. He sat down opposite Prisoner B. Before him on the table he placed a fat dossier, which he proceeded to leaf slowly through.

Prisoner B was made nervous by this procedure, and alarmed by the comfort of the armchair. He longed to sleep.

Suddenly darting a glance at his prisoner, the interrogator

said, "You are looking a touch pale. Not been sleeping too well lately? Would you like a cup of tea?"

In the prisoner's mind rose a vision of a cup of tea in all its benison. He agreed eagerly. "Dick" nodded encouragingly but, doing nothing further, again immersed himself in the dossier.

"I see here that you are fluent in Pashto, Baluchi, and Urdu?"

"No, I'm not. I know a few words of Urdu."

"In what language did you converse with Osama bin Laden?"

Such disconcerting questions made him stutter. "I didn't— I never—I never spoke—I never met—bin Laden when he was alive."

With a supercilious smile, the interrogator said, "You could hardly be suspected of speaking to him once he was dead." He returned to his burrowing in the dossier.

"So, Paul, would you like to tell me something about your life?"

The man's mild tone, his seeming friendliness, released something in the prisoner, released a torrent of speech he could hardly check.

Paul began talking about his father's arrival in England, years ago. Maybe twenty-five years. No, twenty-four. He spoke good English and grew to love England, with its mild, reasonable politics and climate. His wife never accepted that she had left Uganda, made no effort to learn the language. He divorced her and kicked her out.

His father then married an Englishwoman, Gloriana Harbottle, who soon gave birth to Paul. Gloriana demanded too much of her husband. She made him feel inferior. He took to drink and became brutal.

Paul dressed like an English boy. Integration was encouraged. His mother defended him from his father. He was bidden to respect English justice. He was sent to a good school, where he was mercilessly bullied and teased. The other boys called him "Insane Hussein." But he learned his lessons, later procuring a decent job in a law office, where he—

"I don't know when that cup of tea is coming," said the interrogator absently, cutting into the flow of reminiscence.

The prisoner, hurt, fell silent before continuing. "It was in that solicitor's—"

"I see here you were suspected," the interrogator said, without looking up from the page, "of being brainwashed, so that without your knowing it you were in reality a compulsive killer—a latent killer awaiting the signal to kill . . ."

"That is utter rubbish. I am completely normal."

The interrogator looked up. He gestured, raising an eyebrow, saying in a reasonable tone, "But surely not completely normal. Your medical records show a split-personality syndrome. What they call multiple personality disorder."

So they had his medical records . . . He said, "I am not a killer. Far from it."

"Oh, I accept that. It's a laughable suggestion. Someone must have been watching a DVD of *The Manchurian Candidate* one too many times!" He chuckled.

Paul felt that here at last was someone on his side. "The— what used to be called a 'split personality' is actually a help to me as a writer."

"Oh? So when did you first have sexual intercourse with this Irishwoman, Doris McKay, or whatever her name was?"

He was startled, shocked. "That has nothing to do with it!"

"And you fucked her sister, I believe."

"Certainly not."

"Have you been circumcised?"

"Why are you asking me this?"

"How frequently did you have anal congress with this woman?"

"What's this all about?"

"I understand she disliked the flavor of your semen."

He tried to stand up but it proved not so easy. "These bloody questions!"

Dick became furious. "You dare raise your voice to me! Why do you suddenly refuse to answer my questions? I thought we were getting along well, establishing rapport, as it were. Now you dare take advantage of my—"

"Oh, I don't have to—"

"What's this? You are contradicting me now? Just when I was trying to help you? You ungrateful swine!" He banged his fist on the desk. "Records show you to be a ruffian of the first order! Guard!"

The guard appeared with astonishing promptitude.

"Charlie, take this blackguard and lock him up in one of the basement cells."

Paul cried, "Look, I'm sorry, I didn't mean—"

"You Muslims are all the fucking same!" Dick shouted. "Ungrateful pigs!"

"Come on, sonny boy!" said the guard, propelling the prisoner forward by the neck.

THE BASEMENT CELL was small and dark. Its walls were slimy. Its floor was slimy. A stink of vomit prevailed. Something came crawling over the prisoner's body and he shrieked. It scampered off. He supposed it was a rat. And there were other rats. He heard them running here and there. They ran across his legs.

It seemed the rats had fleas. Or the last miserable wretch to be shut in here had left some of his fleas behind. There were other things, too. Crawling or flying. Gnats hummed by his ear.

Suddenly an overhead light came on, blindingly bright. Someone down the end of the corridor had switched on the light—not out of kindness, but so that he could see the filth that surrounded him. The vomit lay in a corner, mainly green and streaked with blood. The rats were at it. They flinched for a moment at the light and then went on with their feast.

As Prisoner B scrunched himself up against the opposite wall, a large cockroach ran from under his heel. It scuttled away, took a swift turn, and disappeared under the cell door. A mosquito, flying blind, came too near. He scrunched it against his forehead.

His whole body itched. He was in the kingdom of the insects.

And the cell was chillingly cold.

SLEEPING IN THE TREES was chillingly cold.

Initially, he chose a tree which had a creeper climbing over it, covered in little fruits like pearls. The creeper grew from the ground, twisting around the trunk of the tree and ascending into its very tops. It was the season for the small fruits. Fremant tasted one, but the flavor was repugnant. With dawn, the fruits shone like teardrops.

He regarded the creeper as a parasite and took some trouble to haul its many stalks out of the branches of the tree. Finally the strands were all cleared away and lay in a pile nearby. The tree immediately began to die. By the next Dimoff, it had fallen, rotten, to the ground.

One day he awoke at sunrise, shivering. Looking down from the rough platform he had constructed in a tree, he saw the ground overnight had become covered with wild irises which were just bursting into pristine bloom, coloring the landscape with their purple-blue flowers. Each opening bud contained a blue-tinted grub.

Although he wondered if the irises exuded poison if you touched them, he climbed down and crouched among them, still shaking with cold. He listened, all senses alert. He caught surrounding vibrations. Something like a noise, almost music, came to him. It could be unseen insects. The plants he had taken for irises themselves gave out a low vibration; their petals were crisp and rubbed gently against each other—Fremant assumed to attract pollinators and to shake out the nesting grubs.

Or fractions of those elusive vibrations possibly emanated from his own body. That extra 3 percent of oxygen on Stygia, as compared to Earth, could be affecting his own metabolism. He was burning out more quickly than normal—burning to death. A kind of religious angst overcame him.

He stood up, to find himself ankle-deep in the stridulating purple flowers.

He was filled with wonder for this strange planet—wonder and dread. He was alien to it, and it to him.

Similar worries bedeviled his quest for food: Was this or that berry edible or poisonous? The one fruit he recognized was the clammerdumm, which he had eaten when under Bellamia's care. He thought affectionately of the woman, with her gentle ways.

Rambling about the nearby hillsides, he came on a sheltered gulch. In the gulch stood a strange artifact. A central stake supported a leather tent which rose to a point. Its sides were decorated with symbols. The structure, temporary at best, was in a dilapidated state. Fremant stood for some while staring at it. It reminded him of something he could not trace. At last he went forward, to pull aside the flap of the tent.

A foul smell, the effluvium of a decaying body, assailed him. On the floor lay a small bipedal body in an advanced state of decomposition. Flying things rose up from it, angry at being disturbed. The surface of the body, and its pits as well, seethed with maggots.

He was staring at the remains of a Dogover who had died alone.

He dropped the flap and retreated.

Hunger drove him back into Haven. Bellamia gave him an affectionate welcome and embraced him. "You are welcome in my little nook," she said. Later, he thought about her phraseology.

FOUR

FREMANT GOT A JOB working in a gunmaker's forge, owned by a big blank-looking man whose small boy was in charge of the bellows. The bellows brought the fire to a temperature which made malleable the metal parts necessary for the machining of crude guns. Fremant's job was to shape wooden stocks for the guns. The last man doing the job had just died.

"You got to keep at it," said the gunsmith, by name Utrersin. "Them stocks don't make themselves." He had a thin skull with a hank of black hair that hung over his forehead like grass over a cliff edge.

His boy politely brought Fremant bread and meat every day at midday.

Fremant took a liking to this lad, whose name was Wellmod. He tried to teach Wellmod the elements of procosmology, drawing diagrams in the ashes of the fire with a poker. The boy was interested.

"Here is the system from which we originated, with a G-type

sun. Way over here is another G-type. This is where we are. The distance is vast. We say one thousand and eighty light-years."

"What's a light-year?" Wellmod asked. As Fremant explained, the gunmaker, Utrersin, came over and listened to the explanation.

He mopped his brow. "How did we ever do it? I opted for years in Cryogenic Storage, as they calls it, so I can't make out how old I be. Centuries, in all probability. 'Tis a bit confusing."

Fremant tried to explain that no one had remained physically whole for the long journey; the brain functions and DNA of many people, male and female, had been stored in so-called Life Process Reservoirs. There was no one on the ship for many centuries. Its shell remained empty and airless; only computers and certain androids were functioning. Otherwise, it traveled chill, without atmosphere, the only sounds being the whisper of cybernetic instruments.

"What about me?" Utrersin asked. "Jupers . . . I heard all this before but never did I believe it possible."

"It's what happened. What was planned. Five years before landfall on Stygia, the ship awoke, the LPRs reconstituted people. The PR it was—Process of Reconstitution. A computer bestowed names on us at random. No two people had any relationship together. It was part of the plan. We were exercised to bring us back to physical health. There were exercises, too, for mental health, and those who did not pass examination were simply eliminated. The LPRs had their failures."

Utrersin shook his head slowly. "All that . . . I thought all that was just bad dreams I had."

"We all have bad dreams."

"Uh. Mine are partickler bad."

"The real bad thing was how quickly people divided into various sects. Atheists, technophobes, religious, and so on . . ."

Utrersin said in wonder, "Jupers, so that's how we was born for life here on Stygia . . . No wonder we be such a rum lot . . ."

"I wasn't born on the ship," said Wellmod brightly. "I'm too young for that."

"Back to work," said Utrersin. "I still can't hardly believe what you say."

The boy started bringing Fremant a jelly of the golden busk, which he ate with pleasure. "You children are so well behaved and kind," he said.

Wellmod smiled and nodded his head without answering.

Every evening in the little square, Elder Deselden and Essanits held a service which all attended. An a cappella choir chanted sacred songs, after which dancers danced. Such songs were designed to be understood by the peasant farmers.

> *The seed we put in the land*
> *In ways that we don't understand*
> *Will grow into food we eat—*
> *As God takes us all by the hand*
> *And when our growth is complete*
> *Will lead us on to the Glor-huh-hory Seat . . .*

And one evening after this ceremony, a bench was brought out and a boy tied down on it, his arms spread and strapped down along the bench. Fremant was amazed to recognize the lad as Wellmod. He was then subjected to twelve lashes with a long, springy cane.

Wellmod had been caught stealing busk jelly from a nearby shop. After the beating, his mother led him away.

Now Fremant understood why the children of Haven were so well behaved. They feared punishment.

When the Shawl brought Dimoff again to Haven, a fire was lit in the little square and sacred songs were sung. Elder Deselden preached that the Shawl was passing over them to express God's contempt for his people, and that they should repent their sins.

Since the doctrinal disagreement between Deselden and Essanits, their relationship had become frosty. Essanits still preached on the fringes of Haven, and some came to listen. He claimed that God loved all his children and the Shawl was an expression of his sorrow. Meanwhile, Elder Deselden ordained that a long melancholy dance was to be performed about the central fire.

After this ceremony, Fremant ventured to argue with Essanits. "You merely confuse people's minds, saying that the Shawl is somehow an expression of your god. The Shawl is merely an astronomical fact, like the Sun, like Stygia. It's a physical law. There are only physical laws."

"Fremant, my son, I grieve that you do not let God into your heart. Who do you think ordains the physical laws, if not God?"

They argued for a while. Both Ragundy and Bellamia came and told Fremant to be quiet. Essanits was patient, if disdainful, appearing prepared to argue forever. He said, "My friends, you cling to your foolish ways if you must. God will accept sinners who repent. I have a disagreement with Deselden, so I shall leave Haven and return to Stygia City."

Fremant spoke respectfully but firmly. "It is obvious that the

Shawl and the six broken Brothers are the remains of some kind of cosmic collision. Why do you need to bring God into it?"

Essanits frowned down at the ground before he spoke.

"Remember, God is in everything—even in your disbelief. Remember how we came here. The great voyage here took many many years. We were contained in molecular form in the vats. Only in the last years of that voyage were we reconstituted from the LPRs. Many persons failed to reconstitute properly and died. Time had taken its toll.

"In those years before we hit Stygia, there was much turmoil. Many factions grew up. It was not only weapons that were destroyed. So was much equipment. Captain Calex was powerless to stop the destruction. I was fortunate enough to salvage a disc which explained to me the omnipresence of Almighty God in the universe."

Sighing, Fremant said that there was no proof God existed.

"Not so. You and I, Fremant, are that proof, with our immortal souls." He stood up, thereby signaling an end to the discussion.

"I am needed in Stygia City and have much to do. I shall see how poor, frightened Hazelmarr fares. I shall slip away while the Shawl is still overhead."

Ragundy cursed. "Essanits, you are a fool! You let Hazelmarr go free after you had told him we were going to come here. He probably went straight to the All-Powerful, to curry favor. Even now, Astaroth's army will be preparing to attack us. You will be spared because you are powerful, but we shall be killed."

"Nonsense!" exclaimed Essanits. "You unbelievers are always afraid of something—something that may never happen." And he strode away.

Fremant and Ragundy got drunk that night. "I can never understand how people think as they do," complained Fremant.

With a sweeping gesture, Ragundy said, "You didn't come here by the ship. You're a supernational—a what?—a supernatural entity!"

"I'm as real as you are. Want me to prove it?"

"Why bother?" said his friend. "Action's what we should bother about, not thinking." He took another drink.

Eventually, both of them fell into a troubled slumber.

He was working in a shirtmaker's shop. There was no denying it. The atmosphere was steamy and obscure. Shirts were hanging from lines like giant birds, some red, some black. The owner of the shop was a big fat man with huge side-whiskers and a black beard. His head was bald and shining, as if the hair there had tumbled down to form a sub-chin proliferation of whiskers.

This man held up a shirt dripping from the dyeworks and addressed his staff.

"See this short? We make the tails too long. From now on, make them a hundred and thirty millimeters shorter. Then I make more profit every short we sell."

Fremant heard himself say, "But the Waabees tuck their shirts into their trousers. If you cut our shirts short, they will not stay put in the trousers."

"They will stay tucked in for half an hour." He brought out a huge watch, which he set ticking. "In half an hour these fool buyers are out of the shop." Already people were leaving. The shop itself was changing.

"But, sir, they will never buy another of our shirts!"

"*Short loyalty*, are you saying? Who ever heard of short loyalty?

You buy a short here one day, the next day another short somewhere else. Short loyalty is for the birds." Such loyalty would not last long. It was confusing that in the dream shirts were "shorts."

"I, for instance, always buy our shirts." But he could not see any.

"Maybe you do, maybe you don't, but you work here—which you won't do if you keep on arguing with me. Let me make it clear, I'm the boss."

"I'm speaking in your interest, boss."

"Look, we cut off a hundred thirty millimeters like I say, maybe we start a new fashion. Maybe everyone wants our shorts what are a hundred thirty millimeters shorter than an ordinary short. Like it's the style. Like it's more hygienic. Also it needs one less button per short. That's all told a savings of . . ." He brought out a huge calculator, wound it up, and began doing sums. The figures fell and covered the floor. Fremant kicked them aside. They spelled something, possibly "Astaroth."

"So I make a profit of ten, maybe eleven stigs on each short, We sell a hundred shorts like a week, that's—um, eleven hundred stigs. So maybe I raise also your wages—those of you I haven't sacked." The hanging shirts were shaking with what he thought was laughter.

But someone was shaking him. "Get up," said Ragundy. "There's trouble!"

Fremant struggled to his feet, groaning.

The window of the room in which they slept looked south toward distant Stygia City. What immediately met Fremant's gaze was the frowsy head and shoulders of the gunmaker, Utrersin, who had been tapping on the window from outside. More distantly, more alarmingly, a troop of horsemen was approaching, galloping in the gloom cast by the departing Shawl. In the gray light, it was hard to make out any detail.

Ragundy looked terrified. "It's Astaroth. He's come to kill us, like I said," he cried. "What are we going to do, Fremant?"

Fremant was equally alarmed. Without answering, he ran outside to Utrersin, who stood clutching Wellmod's hand.

Wellmod seemed none the worse for his beating, and was jumping up and down. "Isn't it exciting?" he said.

"More than that." Fremant stared ahead. The horsemen were no nearer, although they were galloping furiously. Some men carried banners. It was impossible to make out the insignia on the banners. Indeed, the whole scene was oddly blurred, perhaps, Fremant thought, because of the departing Shawl.

"They're coming to get you," said Utrersin with a chuckle. "Yer in for it!"

Fremant narrowed his eyes, staring ahead, trying to make out what was happening. The approaching group of men and animals was oddly unclear. As furiously as they galloped, they were not advancing. Nor did a sound come from them, no shouts, no drumming of hooves.

He looked anxiously at Ragundy.

"They're . . . why, they're ghosts!" Ragundy exclaimed.

"No, they're not," said Wellmod. "They're 'lusions."

Utrersin smote his thigh and roared with laughter. "Had you scared, didn't we? Like the kid says, they're 'lusions. They'll fade in a moment, you'll see."

"I could kill you, you bastard," said Ragundy. "You had me really scared."

"I like to see them," said Wellmod. "They're fun."

"You was scared once, but not no more, are you?" said Utrersin.

"I like to see them. First they come, then they don't come."

As he spoke, the cavalry began to fade. In the breath of a moment, the countryside was empty and the charging horsemen were no more.

Fremant plunged his fists into his pockets. He stared at the ground by his feet. He was mystified.

"It's something to do with the Shawl," said Utrersin. "Don't worry about it."

"No, it's not," said Wellmod. "It's them magic dogs hanging about in the valley."

When Fremant asked the obvious question, Wellmod said that when the Dogovers had been slaughtered, some of their dogs had escaped. They were magic dogs. They projected the 'lusion to scare people.

"How could dogs do that?" Ragundy asked contemptuously.

"I don't know, 'cos I'm not a dog."

NOT A DOG BUT HARDLY A MAN. The statement hounded him in his sleep that night. He had been beaten like a dog. Once more, he was imprisoned in the rundown edifice, once more questioned and abused. He was moved to a room upstairs, where another prisoner had died. His body had not been discovered for some days; the room still stank of his death and decomposition.

Paul felt he was nearing the end of his tether. Looking about the room, he saw pale rectangular patches on the grubby, embroidered wallpaper where framed canvases had once hung. A picture, doubtless a contributor to one of the light patches of wallpaper, and one of the last treasures of an earlier day, lay among the rubbish in one corner of the chamber.

Summoning up his energies, the prisoner made himself, after some time, go over to examine the picture. He could see from the back of it that it had been damaged. One side of its ornate gilt frame was missing. As he moved the painting to turn it over, a pair of rats rushed out and disappeared into a nearby hole in the skirting.

The canvas had been slashed, so that a strip of canvas hung down. It depicted a sturdy middle-aged woman in an apron. She was holding out her bare arms to welcome home a tired laborer in a smock, evidently trudging back to their cottage. The cottage was beehive-shaped and thatched. Behind the male figure were little plump hills, shapely trees, a small flock of woolly sheep grazing.

It was evening. The spire of a church showed from behind one of the hills. The sun was about to set behind the hill, spilling a golden radiance over a gospel-generated landscape.

The scene was a vision of pious tranquillity which represented an England as the artist wished it had once been.

The prisoner stared at it with open mouth. He began to sob uncontrollably.

WHEN NOT WORKING, Fremant returned to wandering. He was drawn to the very territory where he believed the phantom cavalry had ridden. Sometimes he crawled on all fours, sniffing the ground. This was where the herb salack grew. He studied it with interest, to find that its tiny purple flower blossomed only for two days, and only one flower per plant showed at a time; then a bud on a nearby plant would burst into flower. In time, the nature of flowering was such that the first plant would receive another turn. During a Dimoff, no flower appeared.

This odd behavior Fremant ascribed to the scarcity of pollinators. The pollinator was more like a beetle than a bee, and a slow flier. It gave an almost inaudible click as it flew.

He buried his face in the low growth, lying full length, and inhaled its fragrance. Lurking in the minty-sweet scent was something oddly pungent, almost a sexual smell. He felt the mystic connection between all life and the soil of a planet. Yet the patch of salack covered only a small area before dying out. Just as there were few pollinators, so there were few microorganisms in the soil to make it viable. From that it followed that life was sparse and strange.

A soft chattering returned his attention back to his surroundings.

Still prone, he looked up to stare into a pair of deep-set eyes, a dark muzzle, and a row of small, sharp teeth set in an open jaw. The face was furry and sharp. Two ears at the back of the skull were raised in an alert manner.

Fremant froze. It was a kind of dog, most likely hostile, and he was in a most vulnerable position.

"Good boy," he said, almost by instinct. "I won't hurt you."

The jaws moved as if in speech and the gentle chattering noises came again. At the same time, the head was cocked to one side as if in interrogation.

It's trying to talk, Fremant thought in surprise. He tried to flick away a curious occlusion of sight. It was as if he experienced a sudden glaucoma. His sight remained clouded.

Tentatively, the creature stretched a leg forward and placed a paw on the man's shoulder. Fremant tried to wriggle backward. It was then he became aware that a second animal stood at his feet. It uttered something that sounded like a command. Fremant stopped wriggling.

"Well? What are you up to? Are you going to attack me?"

He could not understand, staring through the cloud in his sight into that strange face—animal, yet also, in the concentration of its stare, aligned to human and to insect. He struggled against its chatter, becoming confused.

Slowly, a white shelf unrolled itself before his vision. It was made of an indeterminate material, featureless and flat, dull and matte. As he watched it extend, he saw small stones appear to dimple its surface, each immeasurably distant from the other.

In his bafflement, he knew he was experiencing synesthesia. If this doglike thing was attempting to communicate with him, he could perceive the stimulus received by one sensory system only in a different sensory mode. In the extreme incompatibility of systems, sound became transformed to vision. It was an ultimate in alienation.

Moved by a xenophobic impulse, he sprang up onto his knees and hit the dog-thing on the jaw. It gave a yelp and fled. Its companion ran off with it. Slowly the illusion of endless white shelf faded from Fremant's brain. Slowly, he could see normally again.

From that moment on, his fear of the unexplored planet became submerged in the wonder of it.

HE COULD NOT STOP TALKING about this experience, mainly to young Wellmod. Ragundy was mocking. Utrersin could merely scratch his head and say, "We know what we know. We do what we do." It was Wellmod who said, with a sigh, "These dogs have drawn something from their long insistence—no, I mean existence—here. If only we could unnerstand their commucations, we might learn something."

"You say 'drawn something.' So you think they have intelligence of a kind?"

"Unless what they perjected on you was a kind of dream. That doesn't mean intelly gents, does it?"

"Well, intelligence at least of a basic kind. Anyhow, it wasn't like a dream. At least not the kind of dreams we have. It was—what's the word?—it kept on being the same. Sustained. Not like a dream is . . ."

Utrersin said, "It's no use going on talking like this. It don't help."

"But we have to know," said Fremant.

"Why, when the thing has buggered off?" said Ragundy in his jeering way.

Fremant rounded on him.

"It's important, you fool! Why can't you see that? This alien thing was trying to get in touch with me. To speak to me. So I believe. We're stuck here on this planet and we know almost nothing about it. It has a long prehistory, it has a biomass—about which we know nothing. What are we doing but fooling around, fighting one another? We should be trying to come to terms, to an understanding, with the planet we live on."

Ragundy jeered. "Okay, wise guy, so you sock this animal on the jaw! You're as bad as the rest of us."

· · ·

FREMANT AND BELLAMIA lived uncomfortably in one partitioned room, with Ragundy living next door. They had a low-ceilinged attic room over the forge, where Wellmod also lived, in a few square feet allocated by Frereshin, the owner of the building.

"I can't think why you go on about this vision business," Bellamia told Fremant over their meager supper. "I reckon it was nothing to do with this dog-thing, nothing at all. I reckon you had a sort of an attack. You know, a stroke. A seizure."

"That's rubbish, my dear. It was the dog, a Dogover's dog. Maybe not a dog at all."

"So what was it if it weren't a dog?"

"That's exactly what I want to find out. I regret I hit it. I was so startled, I just struck out."

She waved her spoon at him. "You know that Astaroth had all the Dogovers wiped out, wiped right out. You seem to have forgotten that."

"Yes, yes . . . But one or two dogs ran off and escaped."

Bellamia threw up her arms in despair. "Oh, you'd argue the hind leg off a jackrat!"

Then silence fell. Having finished the meal, Fremant rose to leave the table. Bellamia, who had been frowning, lifted a cautionary finger. "Yes, two dogs! All them horsemen galloping, spread out. So they dogs was comm—comm—what's that word you use, Fremant, love?—commpunicating with each other."

He was impressed. "You're right. Yes! They were communicating together. Their version of talking. If only we could understand . . ."

He bedded down on his straw-filled mattress and was immediately asleep. He was in another world, undergoing torture. Someone was crawling over him.

"Come on, Free, love, wake up." She was thrusting herself against him. "You'd need a dog at each end, like you need two people to hold a long banner, two at least."

He felt her warmth and her aroma. He remained only half-awake. "But the horsemen . . ."

"I dunno. Maybe they got them from your mind. Since they got this mental power?"

"Oh, this bruddy planet . . ." He turned on his side, away from her. She seized her opportunity and more than that. His response was immediate.

"Get into me, will you?" she whispered. "I'm not that old, am I? Besides, it's dark, so you can't tell." She still smelled of salack, and something darker.

"Bluggeration, Bellamia, get off me! I'm tired."

"Come on, rouse yourself, love! You're a man, aren't you? What's this you've got here? Dearie, I could suck it! Just do me, will you? I'm dying for it. What harm can come of it?" She pulled him back against her, coaxing one of her ample breasts into his face, while rubbing her body against his.

He felt himself getting interested. "Rather than argue . . ."

"Ohhh, that's more like it." She opened her legs. "Much more like . . . ohhh, I'd forgotten . . . ohhh . . ."

He gave in to his senses and entered her.

And so the night passed, not unpleasantly.

The repercussions of that night, however, proved difficult to deal with. When Fremant looked at Bellamia by daylight, he thought her old and frumpy, and wondered how he had enjoyed so greatly what they'd done. He felt himself tainted. And yet . . . He breathed in her teasing aromas. She herself was subtly changed. Her face was dreamy on the pillow, and held the beauty of satiety.

"Oh, my sunny sugar stick . . ." she breathed. He loved her as a human being. He had yet properly to value closeness.

Not only did he love Bellamia, he became something of her slave because of those lips that could not speak, that mouth without a tongue, which yet in its enfolding ecstasy met him in an exulted state of feeling. No sooner did he slide his hand down to touch its rough, hairy coating than the secret lure in all women cast its spell upon him, making him mindless with desire.

In the following days, Bellamia did her hair differently. She seemed to tread more lightly. She wore a mysterious smile. He knew from her embrace how womanly she was. He felt again the pervasive healing power of a woman's satisfaction. She had ceased her continuous chewing of the herb salack. She slept in his bed as a matter of course.

She clung to him, even when he didn't want it.

He fended her off. "You make me feel human, dearest," Bellamia said. "I somehow never felt this human before, never before."

"Don't be silly!"

"Can't you say nothing more loving than that, you poor fool?"

He thought she was right. He was a poor fool.

"Is love a silliness?" She kissed him smackingly. "Then silliness is sub—surblime. Tell me again how we came to be on the starship. So little do I know . . ."

Fremant confessed he did not know the scientific details. He said that the great ship, the *New Worlds*, had traveled for many years, at first through a wormhole and then at near-light speeds. In all that time, the starship was empty, empty of human life. Only a few androids worked on its decks, maintaining services.

DNA patterns of many people were filed away in a vitaputer. There were also what were popularly known as "flesh banks," which contained a slurry of stem cells, biochemicals, proteins, and fats. In the last few years of the long voyage, as the ship was decelerating on its approach to the Stygia sun, individual DNA codes were imprinted into the life-matter of the flesh banks. LPR made them alive again, reconstituted. Humans of various ages were produced, new-minted, and trained to be ready for landing on the new planet.

"So I can't really grasp it all, but I was right not to feel human," Bellamia said. "Oh, kiss me again, do! Again a kiss . . . Let me linger, linger ever . . ."

He kissed her. As he turned on his heel to go, he said, "We're human right enough. We brought that from the planet Earth. What we did not bring were all the various organizations, the web of relationships which had been built up between groups of people and nations."

Bellamia called after him, "Where did you get all that wisdom? It explains a lot!"

He could have admitted that he had heard Astaroth say those very words; but why give the bastard any credit?

He had asked her why she was away so much. He felt he wanted her near him. Bellamia said she worked for a man who made clothes, a hermit who lived above the potter's shop in the square.

"What do you do there?" Fremant asked, with a touch of jealousy.

"I make clothes, of course."

"Oh? What else?"

She told him she had contrived a way to weave the wool of goats and sheep-things into a mat. She smiled proudly as she explained, but he was not really interested.

While Fremant labored over his gun stocks in the forge, sweating in the heat of the fire, another fire burned within him, as he conjured up his intimacies with Bellamia.

If the gunsmith noticed these subtle changes, he said nothing. He was a simple and closed man—for which Fremant was grateful.

But more hostile eyes spied on the new intimacy and chose to mock.

"You're shagging that fat lump, aren't you?" said Ragundy with a snicker.

Fremant threw a punch at his face, but Ragundy dodged and struck back, landing a glancing blow. Fremant flung himself at the other, punching savagely. Ragundy coiled an arm about Fremant's neck and they fell struggling to the ground, snarling and fighting.

"Oh no!" cried Bellamia. "My darling, stop, you'll get hurt!"

They were outside, on rough ground. Utrersin came out from the forge with a tub of dirty water. He flung it over the two fighters.

"No brawling! Get up, the pair of you!"

They stood up, sheepish now.

"You started it," said Ragundy, with a sulky glare at his opponent.

"Never mind that," said Utrersin sharply. His eyes gleamed below his overhanging hair. "Clear out, you!"—to Ragundy, who slouched away. "I know a troublemaker when I sees one."

He said to Fremant, "Get inside, you ruffian. There's someone coming. Visitor."

He pointed into the distance.

In the thin sunlight, about a mile distant, a horseman could be seen. Man and horse were moving slowly up an incline. Their figures were sometimes obscured by stubby trees. Yet they came on, steadily approaching Haven.

"Get a gun, load it, stand ready," said Utrersin.

"There's only one of them. Could be it's another of those mirages."

The smith repeated the order. "Get a gun, load it, stand ready."

Fremant did as he was told.

Bellamia had been standing by. "A woman's never wanted. It's a man's world, I fear, a man's world. But I love you so, dear Free. You've changed my life. You'll get yourself hurt, that much I know, and then I'll die. Absolutely die!"

He gave her an affectionate glance. "Quiet, my dear. It's all right."

"Oh no, it's not all right, not at all all right."

Utrersin was looking over the sights of the gun at the approaching horseman.

"Bluggeration!" he exclaimed. "It's a woman!"

Bellamia clutched Fremant's bare arm, sinking her nails into his flesh. "Damn her—she's coming for you, you rat!" Tears stood in her eyes.

Now the rider and her steed were on level ground and moving faster. This was no illusion. The woman had a scarf over the lower part of her face as a protection against dust. Fremant could not recognize her; nevertheless, he had a guess as to who it might be. He breathed faster, with a mixture of excitement and unease.

"Put your gun down," he told Utrersin. Shaking off Bellamia's hold on him, he went forward to meet the rider. Bellamia lumbered off and climbed the steps to their room.

As he suspected, it was Aster, Aster riding a black horse. She entered Haven at a canter. After bringing her mare to a halt, she dismounted, patted the creature, then clutched Fremant's hand.

Although she was out of breath, she began talking rapidly, gazing into his eyes. Her hood and veil had been abandoned.

"I hope you are half as glad to see me as I am to see you. I dreamed one night you were dead, and took it as an omen. I feared for you as I feared for myself. Everything has gone wrong."

"Aster, why are you here?"

Without answering him directly, she continued: "Things are very bad in the city, and getting worse day by day. There's bound to be an uprising. The Clandestines, various factions . . . Ameethira is dead. People got to hear of it. Astaroth beat her to death in an insane rage. I was imprisoned. One of the guards helped me escape—"

"Hold on!" said Fremant. "I can see you are exhausted, Aster. Come inside and sit down. Wellmod will look after your steed."

Meanwhile, Bellamia was coming down their steps, wearing a colorful garment over her shoulders.

Aster took a closer look at Fremant, waving her hands in gestures of rejection.

"You're ill. Filthy. What's happened to you?"

"Never mind that. I have been in a fight."

She threw up her hands. "Ever violent . . . The guard was young and kind. I gave myself to him. When I found Ameethira was dead, I cried and cried. She may really have been my mother for all I know . . ."

Aster took Fremant's arm and, chattering on, began to walk with him toward the cottage. But Bellamia seized her other arm and stopped her. The older woman's face was pale. She loomed over the new visitor.

"You cannot come here and possess him," she said. "We are of different generations, but I cleave to this man. He means much to me. You must understand that clearly."

Aster was disconcerted, as she was meant to be—not least by the colorful woven garment Bellamia wore draped over her shoulders. Bellamia had woven it herself from the wool of goats, and dyed it.

"But—" began Aster.

"Oh, look here—" began Fremant.

But Bellamia was speaking. "It's a sorry place, this Haven is. Those of us of the older generation, who were made up in the ship's factories—PR'd, did they call it?—none of us have any relatives. Old and lonely, we are. No family. No relations—no sisters, mothers, daughters, brothers, fathers. No parents, imagine! So we cling like to a straw to what—to who we love. You can't come over here and just take him from me!"

She glanced at Fremant to see if she had his support. He gave no sign.

Suddenly weary, Aster faced her. She spoke without rancor.

"Let me tell you this, woman—there's no great—what's the word?—there's often pain in having relations. No one would wish for a father such as I have had. He has wounded my life. That's why I need Fremant—brute though he has been to me, in the past now gone."

"Oh, Jupers!" exclaimed Fremant. "Must we be at odds? What is it? Can't you two women be friendly? The miseries of life—the miseries—" He could not find the words.

"There's a room over the pottery where you can sleep," Bellamia told Aster. "You will be safe there. The potter man's not much of a male."

Clouds meanwhile had begun to gather. A heavy rain started to fall.

"Come inside, all of you!" bellowed Utrersin. "You'll drown standing there."

ASTER WASHED AND RESTED. Finally, when she had eaten some bread and a shred of meat, she spoke of what was happening in Stygia City. Fremant and Bellamia sat and listened, with Utrersin and Wellmod restless in the background.

First Aster spoke of the uprising of the Clandestines under Habander. Under cover of Dimoff, they had assembled outside the Center, had killed two guards and set fire to the building. A new Clandestine leader—Habander having been deposed—had led a contingent into the offices. His party was armed with swords. They met opposition and a desperate struggle took place on the stairs and an upper landing. The leader was badly wounded before the opposing force was overcome. Astaroth, meanwhile, made his escape from the burning building by way of a back stair. He had not been seen since. A search was in progress when Aster escaped and made for Haven.

Essanits had taken charge and was trying to bring order back to the city as Aster left.

"As you know, I had little respect for the Clandestines," said Fremant. "What caused them to act so boldly?"

"Oh, I forgot to tell you!" said Aster, flapping her hands. "This is really the most important thing: A message came by light-drone from Earth. Seems things are better there now, at last. I mean, things are less unlawful, I think. The Earth government—it, what?—oh, it *rejects* the philosophy of the WAA. That's the philosophy which guided it for so long."

Fremant was listening with interest, while taking in Aster's body language. She spoke hurriedly, continually waving her hands. Those hands waved uselessly before her, stressing no points, illustrating nothing, a mere nervous gesturing. "Her fluttering emotional life," he thought to himself.

Aster continued: "According to this message, Earth government now claims that the wiping out of the Dogovers on Stygia was illegal. Not lawful. It is pronounced to be—what is that word they used? Juice? Cider? No, got it—genocide." The hands fluttered like captive doves. "Under Astaroth, my father, as you know, under him genocide was committed. So he had to be arrested. But he has disappeared. Disappeared. No one knows where to . . ."

"How could a message come from Earth?" asked Utrersin, the gunsmith. "That's all bunkum."

"It's true, it may have been a forgery. Why was it sent to the Clandestine group?" Aster asked.

Fremant commented, "You remember Captain Calex on the ship? A good man. Some said he was a cyborg or an android. He wished Stygia to be a peaceful and happy planet—unlike the hellhole it has become. As bad as Earth . . ."

The others discussed the new turn of events for a while.

"This could mean better times for all," said Bellamia.

Fremant said, "But now Essanits is in command? Essanits was the leader who finished off the last of the Dogovers. Why isn't *he* under arrest—him and all his men?"

Aster said, "Unless the situation has changed since I left, Essanits was pardoned because he has become very holy. He confessed his sins and has vowed to make a rest—no, arrest—no, a *restitution.*"

Utrersin butted in. "What's that word mean? Never heard it before. Will it bring back to life all the Dogovers we killed?"

WORD SOON SPREAD THROUGH HAVEN that the harsh regime in Stygia City had collapsed. With Essanits in command, conditions would undoubtedly improve everywhere. Celebrations began. Women started to dance in the little square, and one of them sang a song of rejoicing.

> *Cry no more, ladies, no reason to mourn!*
> *Cry no more, ladies, a new day will dawn.*

Liddley did not dance or sing. She stood apart, arms akimbo. Fremant stared at her with some remorse. She had no child at her breast. Evidently the baby with the fixed and dreadful grin he had seen her nursing had died.

A rumor circulated that Essanits would soon return to Haven, and some even said that he would bring with him more men to work in the fields.

Elder Deselden appeared, walking with a staff and escorted by two imposing young men. He cried out, stopping the dancing and singing.

"Be ashamed, all of you! There is no cause for rejoicing. Violence has broken out in the city, good men have died. Now Essanits is in control, we hear. One bad man has gone and another has taken his place—that's all. Do you not remember that when Essanits was here he preached a poisonous creed? Let us hope and pray he never comes back and leaves us in peace! Return to your homes, good people."

So the day's routine was resumed, a struggle for many, who perforce went into the fields, bending their backs, straining their sinews. Old men died. Babies cried to be fed. Rain came down. The six fragmentary Brothers streamed overhead through the night, going somewhere, getting nowhere.

Fremant still lay with Bellamia. He felt her smooth skin and the contrasting rough texture of her woven shawl.

"It reminds me of something."

"What can it remind you of?" she asked.

"I can't tell . . . Something we've lost."

She would have none of it. "Be grateful for what you've got. You've got me."

One man brought in the skull of a dog-thing. His spade had struck it, together with another skull in less good condition.

Some looked at the skull with idle interest, not inquiring. Some went out to the laborers' field and found there a veritable cemetery choked with dog-thing skeletons which a recent flood had revealed. These were the remains of exoskeletons, punctuated here and there by small oblong holes along their sides.

"Them Dogovers was mighty fond of their old dogs, I'd say," said a gatherer. His remark was received by the others as significant. Work had to go on. No more inquiry was made. The skeletons were broken up.

Then came a wondrous day when a pervasive humming was heard.

Nobody was keen on new things. They looked to the sky in dread. A flimsy bird made of canvas and string and wire circled high above the roofs of Haven, uttering its throaty noise.

Workers in the fields straightened their backs to gaze upward. In wonder, men who had never left their village since they left their ship gazed upward. Small boys minding goats shielded their eyes and gazed upward. Utrersin left his forge and gazed upward.

"This can't be good," he muttered.

The strange machine came lower. So low that the wind could be heard whistling in the wires, above the engine noise. The watchers on the ground could plainly see a man, a pilot, crouching in the wooden body, and propellers front and back, moving the artificial bird through the air. Now the bird was near to land, no longer rushing, seeming almost to hesitate before descending to a stretch of level ground. There it ran a little way, slowing, and the onlooking boys began to cheer and run toward the strange machine—when it struck a boulder and overturned. Almost gracefully, the canvas wings arced above the body, hit the ground, and folded, while the tail and body seemed to disintegrate and fell into the field.

A roar rose from the villagers. Now they had a part to play in the drama and ran to the wreckage to see what had happened to its pilot.

Fremant was among those who discovered the body sprawled in the long grass below a section of crumpled canvas. He helped to drag the man free.

"He's dead!" the cry went up. Together with "He's black!" — this in a different key.

They carried him to the nearest cottage, laying him reverently in the shade under the steps. Whereupon he sighed, gulped, and sat up. Women in the crowd clapped. Some cried.

Fremant recognized the pilot. "It's Chankey!" he exclaimed. Chankey, the winner of the Kontest Fremant had refereed in Stygia City. A cheer went up from all concerned.

Someone helped Chankey to his feet. A woman brought him a clay cup full of water, which he drank.

EVENTUALLY, WHEN FULLY RESTORED, the stalwart Chankey told his story.

"What a struggle it has been . . . It was the light-drone from Earth that began it . . . Fortunately, Safelkty got to it first . . . that scientific man . . . Else it would have been destroyed . . ." Chankey spoke in gasps, leaning against a cottage ladder.

"That's not the same story what we heard," said Ragundy.

Chankey took another drink of water and appeared to recover more fully from his rough landing.

"Earth has 'clared the killing of the Dogovers who lived here before us jennyside. That word means the delib'rate killing of a whole race. So revolt broke out. Astaroth's regime is smashed.

Astaroth has disappeared. Essanits has taken control, appointing Safelkty as his Director of Science."

"Never mind all that history," said one villager. "Tell us what is this flying thing you come here in."

"Is there news of my father, Astaroth?" asked Aster.

Speaking carelessly, Chankey said, "I did hear someone say he crossed the lake and cut Habander's throat, but who knows?"

"But this flying thing!" some villages repeated.

"Ah, it's Safelkty's first invention," said Chankey proudly. "It's called a 'push-pull.' One whirler in front, one in back. At last, we humans have conked the air!"

"And you hit the ground," said Utrersin mockingly.

"You primitive folk here have no decent land to stop on," said Chankey. "Life is going to be different now. I have come in advance, but soon Essanits and his force will be here to address you. Safelkty has plans to build a proper road from Stygia City to Haven, with horseless—um, machines—to run on it. Your lives are going to change, I'm proud to say to you!"

This speech drew varied responses from the crowd. Certainly there were those who welcomed the idea of change, and cheered vociferously. The majority, however, feared that any change would be for the worse; that, for instance, their own affairs would be ruled from afar, to their disadvantage. For what did Stygia City know or care about Haven?

Even those who had previously complained most vocally about the shortcomings of life in their poor little village suddenly found in their hearts a new love of the place as it was, and booed accordingly.

Change! Machines that fly! Terrible!

FIVE

CONTROLLER ALGERNON GIBBS—ALGY to his enemies—sat alone in his office in the Ministry. He had locked his door so as not to be disturbed. Grim files stood imprisoned on shelves. The one window was barred and locked. He was still suffering from the humiliation of Abraham Ramson's visit.

As part of his tour of inspection of British ministries, Ramson had convened a meeting of Gibbs's team of interrogators. He had complained about almost everything, from the dilapidation of the building and the amateurism of the interrogations to the dearth of ice in the catering department. Without mentioning Gibbs's name, he had lowered him in the estimation of the listeners. Gibbs had shown the American, on leaving, to the stretch limo awaiting him before he retired to his office, in a bad mood. He sat scratching his designer stubble.

He called for his secretary. Agnes Sheer emerged from an inner room. She was tall and elegant, clad in gray—two inches taller than Gibbs, for which he resented her.

He tossed her the disc which Ramson had presented to him on their frosty parting.

"Open that," he said.

Sheer slipped the disc into the computer. A picture lit almost immediately on the big wall screen. HEAVY QUESTIONING, it announced. It was followed by ENEMY ENQUIRY DIVISION and an eagle.

It then ran through an array of sophisticated interrogation aids. There were illustrations with brief descriptions, and an order number opposite each.

"Shut it down," Gibbs said. Sheer shut it down.

"We are so much worse funded than the Americans," Gibbs said. "It's a bloody nuisance. How could we afford the Thresher, or those electric shoes?"

"Perhaps we could get them cheaper through our Chinese dealer," Sheer suggested.

He ignored her remark. "We might order some of those posters. They should sap morale."

"Now?"

"Now."

When the woman had left, Gibbs turned with a sigh to the book on his desk. He opened it to page 125.

He removed his glasses, polished them, then reapplied himself to reading the text of *Pied Piper of Hament*, by Paul Fadhill.

<<The next place to visit at the fairground was the Wonderworld booth. By then, both Harry Marigold and Celina Celandine were a little worse—or better, as the case might be—for drink.

In the booth, it was dark. Something glittered. Something tittered. The tittering something proved to be a witchlike old lady in a bonnet and an avaricious mood. She was pacing to and, consequently, fro. She demanded that her palm should be—no, not crossed—*loaded* with silver.

When this had been accomplished, she ordered the loving pair to sit on a rickety sofa. It certainly had rickets in its legs. "A mystical island for you?" she croaked.

"Oh yes, Bali, please!" the duo said in chorus.

"Better than Bali, my dearies!"

"Where's better?"

"Place where everyone is stoned. Heh heh heh."

She waved her palsied old hands over them, chanting in an unknown tongue as she did so.

"*Obi chagit hocha hanka heegi abrogal dimkey dimkey dormug gé abeagle ga . . .*"

Next second, it seemed, the duo were standing in an enchanted place. It was as neat as a model, every blade of grass in place, little deer sauntering, white doves winging, a pure white gazebo gazing—one like snow, the other more like milk—by a stream curling down from a hill with slopes as gentle as a woman's breast. A wonderful parklike countryside surrounded them, bounded by a silver sea.

"So that's where our silver went!" Harry exclaimed.

"Hush! Someone's coming."

And someone was certainly stomping along towards them—a big grey man. Celina was alarmed.

"Oh, hi! Nice place you have here. I trust we are not trespassing, sir?"

The big man ground to a halt. He was made entirely of

stone, down to his stone underpants and beyond. His face was as animated as one of the faces on Easter Island, though without the same sophistication of expression. When he opened his mouth to speak, smoke came out, with a glimpse of fire behind. The smoke formed the shape of an equilateral triangle before dispersing into the pure air.

He took hold of their arms, one arm in each of his rough stone hands, and led them along. He emitted smoke instead of conversation, but there is nothing witty one can say to a series of equilateral triangles once one has agreed about the square of the hypotenuse.

The stone man took them to Stone People Village, where they were kindly treated. They lived in a stone house with a stone cat. There were stone curtains at the windows. They slept in a stone bed. They sat on stone chairs to eat at a triangular stone table.

Fortunately, the food was real food. They dined as do the wealthy of Hampstead, on plates of aubergine and calves' liver, sprinkled with coriander, served with basmati rice, and doused in balsamic vinegar, with Madegasca prawns for a side dish. These platters were followed by *crème brûlée* and plum pudding in a suet crust with lashings of Jersey cream.

As they were enjoying themselves, they were—strange as it might seem—following a different and dual existence in another world, where Harry Marigold worked in a pharmacy dispensing prescriptions and Celina Celandine designed outdoor clothes for a fashionable couturier who lived in the neighbouring mosque.

They were puzzled by this double life and met secretly to

plot their escape from it, walking in a nearby park, peaceful except for traffic continually roaring by.

"It's metaphysical," said Celina. "In fact, metafizzicle, like a bottle of newly opened San Pellegrino."

Harry agreed. "No good asking my boss about it. He's too thick, although he's shockingly thin. He's the sort of guy who thinks that endorphins are a kind of fish."

They were laughing together as they strolled through the park, where no one could overhear their jokes—or understand them, indeed, if they caught the odd punch line head-on.

Said Celina, "The bloody government is no help at all."

Harry said, "What we need to do is blow up the Prime Minister. That would solve our problems."

"I can see it now," Celina said, laughing. "Bits of him spread all over Downing Street."

"Yes—to be known thereafter as Downer Street . . ."

She took his arm. "Or we could cast the devil into a bottomless pit."

He patted her behind. "Better still a pitiless bottom."》

Algernon Gibbs grew tired of this whimsy. His thoughts began to wander. He lit a cigarette. Only one more left in the pack. "Sodding job this . . . Too noisy . . . Not enough freedom, for a start . . . Promotion . . . Deserve a sodding knighthood . . . Could get another job with less strain . . . Train horses. Geld them . . . Castrate grown men . . . Must come off these sleeping pills . . . Become a transvestite. Men admiring . . . Change my name . . . Celina. Not bad . . . Celina Gibbs. Gibbs Girl Gives It! . . . Sodding great bosoms . . ."

As his thoughts drifted by, thoughts often rethought, his left hand held the cigarette. It was cork-tipped. His pale, cruel right hand unzipped his trousers and, reaching in, began to play with what it found there. What it found there showed signs of life. Celina Gibbs. Pride of Pinner . . . Pretty as a picture . . . Prettier, prettier . . .

The rimless glasses began to mist as his breathing became heavier.

THE CLOUD COVER was becoming heavier. A cool breeze blew. People coughed, spat phlegm on the parched ground.

The crowd milled about, not knowing what to do. The venerable Elder Deselden hobbled forward with his staff. He was escorted by two young men armed with staves, whom he called his possles. One of his most devoted followers, an old man called Citrane, whose face, with its short beard, resembled a goat's, hurriedly got down on hands and knees, thus providing a stool for the old holy man, who seated himself on this human support and spoke.

"Master Chankey, you arrove here as a disaster from the air. We want no more disasterers here. Our lives are dedicated to religious matters. We want nothing to do with Essanits, nothing to do with your science. We recall how Astaroth, whatever his other flailings, wisely destroyed most of the traces of what we call tick-nologogy, including all metal flying things, sparing only the great ship-thing that brought humanity to this world. We do not want to start up such monstrobities again."

Chankey responded to this speech with some tact.

"Whether or not traveling away from Earth was a sin, I cannot say. But the arid nature of our late leader drove him to destroy much that would have helped us to survive here on this world. He delicated his life to hate and harm, by destroyting all of the so-called Dogovers. As we must make amens for that massy killing, so we seek to resterore the good things that will make our life easier—and your life here in Haven easier."

Liddley stepped forward with a stern face and addressed them.

"All right. You men have had your say. Now I will have my say."

"Shut up!" shouted Ragundy, but Liddley continued unperturbed.

"People in Haven perish. They are accustomed to the process of perishing, of living half a life . . . Our customs and attitudes toward life have developed to fit in with the process. So children die and old people starve and women are overworked. It's undernorrishment . . . That's the trouble. Undernorrishment. So we drink the foul water from our well and die of it. We're too enzausted to clean out our well, imagine!

"This sorry stake of affairs has come about gradually. So we ourselves don't see the full horror of the system. In fact, we regard the system as a natural and proper way of things.

"Now you come here promising machines! What we need is fertilizer and traps for control of the dacoim pests. We need to live decently. Machines are no good to us.

"There, I've had my say, writhe or wrong . . ." She stepped back into the crowd, which was growling, either in agreement or disapproval.

"Wrong!" said Chankey curtly. "How will these traps and things you talk about get here if not by machines?"

It was Fremant who spoke up on Liddley's behalf. "If they all crash like your machine, they won't be much help . . ."

The two possles were closing in on Liddley, swinging their staves, shouting that a woman had no business to speak in public. Fremant flung himself between them and Liddley.

Immediately, the nearest stave was in motion. It struck him on the forehead. He heard someone shriek as he went down. Bellamia and Aster rushed to his aid. Liddley fled.

HE WAS COOLING his throbbing head on the cold parquet floor. Somehow, he knew it was winter. He was wearing only light clothing. He knew he ached all over, and stank. The Ministry had failed to release him. A cockroach came to inspect him.

Disappointment and disgust were upon him. Another personality broke from him, like a playing card falling from a gaming table.

MID-OCEAN, and the great dolphin-driving sea breathed its restless slumber of waves, ocean-blue and unfathomable. This time he was a sailor named Yargos. He was one of a crew who knew only the sounds of the sea, the groan of the wooden vessel that sailed the sea, the crack of cordage and the drumming of the full-bellied sails overhead.

Yargos wore a gold ring through the lobe of his right ear. He was strong, his body well muscled. His thoughts rarely reached beyond the day. He and his shipmates were equals, bound together by the loneliness of their voyage. Matters might change when and if they reached port; but for the present they were companions in defiance of the elements.

By night they lashed the wheel and all slept, except for a man acting as sentry.

Yargos wrapped himself in a rug and slept in the bows. He dreamed of a brown-skinned slave boy in distant Cymantta, a boy with a foreskin like a lady's silk stocking.

The ocean by night underwent a change. The mighty roll of unbreaking waves became luminescent. A million million tiny organisms strove to perpetuate themselves, burning with a cold light as they did so.

High above the mast, high above the ocean, radiated an answering light, where a million million distant suns gave forth their unsleeping signal.

But Yargos found no permanent place to accommodate him within Fremant's psyche. He lived for day after repetitive day before disappearing where no man knew.

HE LISTENED TO THE WAIL of the wind dying. After a while, he opened his right eye. His left eye had been punched and would not open.

He saw about him the familiar stale room, far too large to be called a cell. Its ceiling bore ornate plasterwork, with cupids. To one side was a grand cold fireplace with cupids. He was all too familiar with this room. Understanding had dawned long since in him that his torturers had taken over and occupied a once-grand mansion, a home long ago of fine, possibly respectable, habitation, where people—families—may have lived out their lives in good countenance. Well, that was one guess, guaranteed to add to his misery.

He lay sprawled on the floor, oppressed by the great hollow space around him. All sorts of insects moved about the floor. The place was sinking into decay, and a small despised fauna was taking over. He watched earwigs scurrying, wood lice taking their time.

The prisoner watched a centipede behaving strangely, running into cracks, running out again, its body contorted, running in circles, running into skirting boards. As it fled nearer to him, he saw that a tiny red ant had clamped itself firmly to one of the centipede's antennae. In panic, the centipede rushed about, unable to shake off its minute assailant. In desperation, it fled under a broken strip of planking and the prisoner lost sight of it.

He lay thinking about the poor insect and its terror. Inevitably, it would exhaust itself and die. Then the remorseless ant would drag it away to be consumed.

The absolute horror of all life possessed him.

The relatively civilized England he had known also had its red ant, heralding its destruction.

He knew he had been incarcerated for many weeks, if not months, although they had said they would let him go free. They had not done so yet. They said that certain authorizations were required for his release.

Reflections and regret poured through his mind. In what he had imagined were more civilized days, he had wished to be part of the British mainstream, despite his ancestry, which he mostly despised. He had adopted an English persona as Paul Fadhill.

He had consorted with English friends and had even written what he regarded as an English comic novel.

Now he saw how false had been his persona. He had betrayed himself. Perhaps subconscious knowledge of that betrayal had prompted him to write the few lines about the assassination of the British prime minister, for which he was now being punished.

But who was he? What was he? Where was he? His mind circled around such questions, like a rat investigating a dead body, as the misery of the days went by.

The long wait, punctuated by interrogations that covered the same familiar ground as previously, was gradually eroding his identity, as the identity of the building in which he was incarcerated was being eroded. He whispered his name to himself, cheek pressed against the filthy parquet. "I am Paul Fadhil Abbas Ali, Paul Fadhil Abbas Ali . . . ," over and over.

He faded out, to see the troubled face of—what was her name?—was she the darling Celina?—Doris?—faithful Bellamia?—she lived on what he knew as Stygia—looking down on him. He stretched out a hand to her, though his hand was as cold and heavy as stone. Very slowly the vision faded and he found himself in a dreary solitude.

At some later time, the door of the chamber was thrown open and the two guards entered. Without ceremony, they hauled him to his feet. He was made to walk down the corridor.

"There's news for you," said the younger of the two guards.

He made no answer. He was full of fear. His throat was dry and almost choked him.

He was dragged into one of the interrogation rooms. It had undergone some redecoration since he was last in there. On one wall hung a blown-up photograph of a man suspended by a hook through his back. His head, though not actually severed from his body, hung by a strip of skin against his chest. He was naked. His genitals had been severed.

Underneath the picture, someone had scrawled "Love will find a way."

The room was dark, except for a bright spot which shone into Paul's eyes as he was secured to the chair.

He sat there, unmoving, eyes closed, waiting. After a long wait, a man in heavy shoes or boots entered the room by a rear door. He scraped a chair about and then was sitting, invisible behind the glare of the light, facing Paul across the table.

"You again," he said. Then, with sarcasm in his reedy voice, "Nice to see you again."

Paul made no response. This was not Abraham Ramson. Abraham Ramson was long gone. This was a minion, an English minion. Possibly a youngish man out to make his mark in this vile profession.

"Bit cold today, ain't it?" Spoken in a jeering fashion.

Again, no response from Paul.

"I got a bit of news for you, Ali. What you think it is?" A Cockney or Essex accent.

He managed to say, "Don't know."

"Speak up!"

"I said, 'Don't know.' "

"Slap 'im abart a bit."

A guard duly did the slapping, knocking Paul's head first to one side, then the other.

"Awright. Now wake up. It's a lovely morning outside." He gave a laugh like a bark.

Paul heard the bark, saw nothing behind it, no human form. Only the light blinding him.

"I was up at sparrow fart. How about you, Ali?" More humor. "So, like, what was the name of this book you writ?"

"*Pied Piper of Hament.*"

"How long was you sat there writing it?"

"About a year."

"What was the story about?"

"Life in England. And in a fantasy world. Comedy."

"No, it wasn't. It wasn't no comedy. You're lying. It was about this black bloke married to a white girl. These here guards don't like fucking liars, do you, guards?"

He was hit and kicked. Being strapped in the chair, he was unable to evade the blows.

"So you made a scad of dosh out of this lousy book of yours."

"Not much."

"What nationality would you say you was?"

"I'm English. You have my passport. It says there I'm English."

"So how come you got this weird Islamic name, then?"

"I—it's my father's name. I can have a Muslim name and still be English."

"Then how come you Muslims are trying to destroy our culture?"

He wanted to ask what culture exactly this loathsome minion possessed, but did not dare, for fear of the beating that would surely follow such a remark.

"Muslims, no. Only a few terrorists . . ."

Yet he thought to himself, as the minion started to rant about this and that, that many Muslims had made the mistake of living apart, emphasizing their difference by insisting on dressing differently, on living tribally, on remaining woefully ill-educated, as many had lived for generations in dusty distant villages. Little had changed in two thousand years. Unlike the Hindus, who slipped successfully into British life, many men he knew kept their wives imprisoned in their houses, unable to speak a word of English. He had integrated, had naïvely thought himself English; now he was being disabused.

AND YET . . . ALL PREJUDICE ASIDE, Muslims were right, surely, to disapprove of the behavior of many young English, the binge-drinkers of both sexes, the young women dressed as if ready for immediate promiscuous sex. The display of female navels. The disrespect shown to their seniors.

The minion was saying, "Here's another bit of goo' news for you. Guess what?"

He made no answer. He just wished to die. It was the tiny red ant again.

"I said guess fucking what?"

"Oh god, I don't know. My release has come through?"

"You getting impatient or summing? No, even better than that. This bird what you married, this Doris . . ."

"What about her?"

"Well, she had a bit of a heart attack in here, didn't she?"

"Is she all right?"

"All right? All right! I s'pose you could say that, 'cos she had a lot of convulsions and she pegged out."

"Oh, you wicked wicked bastards . . ."

"It was awful to watch. Her shitting herself. Red in the face, writhing about on th' floor. We couldn't stop laughing . . ."

"Oh. Oh. Oh. Damn you all to bloody fucking hell . . ."

"Take this bugger away, guards. Maybe he'll see the funny side in a bit."

Chuckling at this remark, the guards unstrapped Prisoner B and dragged him away.

Back in his black room, he lay motionless, too choked with sorrow even to cry. The ghastly barbarous injustice of the world . . .

Time passed like the creak of a floorboard under a slow tread. A man called "the Doctor" entered the chamber and stirred him with his foot.

"Ali?"

No response.

"You'll go catatonic, man, if you don't move yourself . . ." He produced a syringe.

A VOICE WAS SAYING, over and over, *"It's a psychotic hallucination, it's a psychotic hallucination, it's a psychotic hallucination, it's a psychotic hallucination,"* on and on.

He could not tell where the voice was coming from.

"Oh, he's coming round at last, I reckon . . ." It was a woman speaking.

She forced a bitter medicine between his lips. He gagged on it.

"There, now, that's better, isn't it, dear?"

"I thought you were dead, Doris, my precious love."

"Who's this Doris you're on about? It's Bellamia. I'm Bellamia. Why don't you rember me?"

"Bellamia . . ."

Later, he sat up. She supported him against her soft body. Breathing was a labor for him. He welcomed her warmth.

"I'll take the bandage off."

"Oh, Bellamia . . . thank you . . . It's Stygia, isn't it? I'm back on Stygia. It's my mind . . ."

He broke into a storm of weeping. He drew his knees up to his face as his whole body shook with his tears, which were extruded with force.

"There, there, you're better now."

"Oh, how can I ever be better?"

She made motherly comforting noises while smoothing the back of his head. "That was some hit you got. Those iggerant swines . . . Now we have to set you on your feet again. There's someone wants to see you."

She helped him to stand and led him to the window. His eyelids retreated into their hiding places of flesh, yet he saw nothing. Only gradually there dawned to his sight a misty view. He could not tell what he was gazing on. He seemed to discern a series of rounded teeth, stacked somewhere among bones, wrapped in a loathsome mist which coiled up from the ground. Where this dreadful vision was located he knew not.

He stared at it in fear, his body still wracked with sobs.

Only gradually did the mist clear, the prospect resolve itself. The rounded teeth became the helmets of soldiers, the bones the staves they carried. And these men stood in the old simple square of Haven, evidently awaiting orders.

He propped himself against the lintel of the low window, panting with relief.

"Oh, dear Bellamia . . . ," he said. "Deformity . . . How did it all happen? Why?"

"There, there, my love!"

Immense gratitude filled him for her tender care of him. He put an arm about her and kissed her cheek.

It took half a day for him to pull himself together again, and then he was led into the presence of Essanits.

Essanits was sitting at a rough-hewn table, concentrating on a small insect-animal. The small creature was balancing on its folded back legs. It was sharp-faced, its upper body covered in a chitinous armor. When Fremant entered, it seemed to take fright and half-curled into a ball, so that the plates of its armor showed clearly. Essanits whispered softly to it and it resumed its normal shape.

Without taking his eyes from the creature, which Fremant recognized as a dacoim, Essanits slowly brought a cage from one side and set it over the dacoim, which scuttled about from one side to another, trying to escape from its imprisonment.

Only then did Essanits look up. "I love this creature, as God loves us," he said sternly, fixing Fremant with his dark regard. "It is intelligent. I do not want it to escape."

"If it loved you back, it would not wish to escape," said Fremant.

Essanits's large, hard face performed a kind of smile, as his large, pale lips spread across his lower cheeks. "You have some authority to say that, Fremant?"

"I know what it is like to be in captivity and to be tortured."

The voice of the other sank by an octave. "I wish only to tame this poor wild thing. Imagine if we could teach dacoims to believe in God . . . We should then have a better world."

He hesitated, wide, pale lips slightly open, before saying, "We have a chance for that better world. You may have considered that since we were reconstituted, we have no nationalities such as caused such trouble on Earth. We are all one nationality, so to speak. That is certainly a positive thing."

Dismissing the subject, he gestured to Fremant to be seated.

"Much has changed since you came to live out your life in Haven, Fremant. The arrogant extremist Astaroth is no more. Reason and science have replaced him and his regime of extreme austerity."

Fremant stared hard at the man sitting opposite him.

"You mean Safelkty? He's the science man, isn't he? You aren't so keen. Is that why you lost the leadership? Is that why you are here?"

Essanits looked down at the table and sighed. Then he lifted his head and said evasively, "I have a mission, in which I trust you will be involved." He rose and went to the door, to summon in Chankey and two other men. These others he introduced as Tragonn and Klarnort, both short, stocky men, clad in leather. They gave Essanits a salute, smiling uneasily.

Rising to his feet, Essanits said, directing his words as much to the two newcomers as to Fremant, "To us is given an honorable task. We have to trek to the land called Incessible, where we understand a small body of Dogovers still survives. We must bring these little Dogovers back to Stygia City, to reinstate them, nourish them, and do everything in our command to make amends for the genocide perpetrated by the previous regime of Astaroth—in which, to my regret, I—I was also involved."

"The journey will cause harmship," said Chankey. "It's your chance to make you feel better—make amens."

"Yes, that's what I said. Hardship." Essanits's lips closed tightly over the word.

"Why can't you go on your lone?"

"Only a small company can get through to Incessible."

He spoke sharply. He turned to Fremant. "Since you have some experience crossing alien territory, we want you to accompany us. You have an obligation to me. I shall be glad to have you with us on the trek—despite the psychotic interludes to which you are subject. We also expect that your friend, Utrersin, the gunmaker, will come with us."

"No, I AIN'T GOING on this mad trek," said Utrersin when approached by Essanits and Fremant. "Why should I? I never killed none of these Dogovers, not like you. 'Sides, Incessible Land, that's far away. You'll never make it there and back. You'll die on the way. You can go, but I ain't going with you."

Essanits wrinkled his brow, but said in his most civil manner, "You must surely feel you have a moral obligation to make restitution to the Dogovers."

"No, I don't feel no moral obligaten at all," said Utrersin, shaking his heavy locks. "I were told not so long ago I had one of these moral obligatens to kill 'em all orf. So much for all such talk. No, boss, I ain't leaving home for any idea of the sort."

He concluded with a snort of contempt, much like a horse neighing—like an image of the prospect he was denying.

"But *I* will go with you, hardshit or not." The words came from the shadowy rear of the shop, where stood Bellamia. She came forward. "Essanits, you need a woman with you. Women have good sense and instinct—better than men. Your expition is stupid because it has no one to nurse these poor little Dogovers. Who can do that better than a woman—a good tough gal like me?"

Frowning, Essanits asked her if she could ride a horse.

"As good as you can!"

Essanits glanced at Fremant, sighed, nodded.

"We get on our way tomorrow."

THE MORNING WAS GRAY, with small scudding shreds of cloud traversing a more general cloud cover. Men and horses cast no shadows. Early though it was, a number of Haven denizens had turned out to watch the small expedition depart.

Essanits was seated on his old black stallion, Hengriss, waiting in silence as the others assembled. Chankey, Tragonn, and Klarnort were armed and each had rolls of bedding strapped to their backs, thus appearing like victims of some strange deformity. Fremant had provided himself with one of Utrersin's guns, but was otherwise unencumbered. Bellamia had lashed a box of kitchen utensils to the rear of her saddle.

As well as these six horses, there were three more, two being packhorses, loaded with canvas shelter, food, fodder, and other necessaries, while the third horse was ridden by the person in charge of the packhorses—Wellmod, now of the age of puberty and defying Utrersin. All these horses were humped, the humps containing their air-tubes. Behind the packhorses came a string of young goats, one tied behind the next, to provide meat on the long journey.

The goats could produce milk and cheese of a low order, and in this way had acquired the name "goat," though in appearance they more resembled something between a beetle and a spider on a large scale. Each creature was long enough to accommodate ten dainty legs. Six of these goats had been rounded up and tethered.

Several people gave advice to Essanits, which he acknowledged loftily. His response was to curl his ample lip, his large face unlit. Liddley came up, to try to persuade Fremant and Bellamia not to leave Haven. Fremant sadly shook his head. He reached down from the saddle to shake her hand in a gesture of farewell.

Elder Deselden looked on from a distance, content to see Essanits leave, but saying nothing.

When Essanits gave the signal, the group moved off in single file. A pale beam of sun penetrated over the hill to encourage them on their way.

For the first kilometer or two, they followed a trail and moved among fields of rydall and peppy dirdist and other vegetables. Solitary men or women stood like scarecrows along the way, armed with sticks to ward off marauding dacoims.

They had almost reached the top of the incline when one of these human scarecrows approached the group. It was a woman, raggedly dressed. It proved to be Aster, who pulled away her customary hood as she seized the bridle of Fremant's horse. She shook it as if in a nervous attack, but spoke in a low voice.

"Fremant, I ask nothing of you. I know you to be a callous brute. I know you care nothing for me. I know you to be a murderer and a rapist. Nevertheless, I ask you, I beg you, to take me with you wherever you go. I must escape this bondage."

He did not dismount. He asked her what she meant by bondage.

"Bluggeration! Did you not hear? Do you know nothing? I was sold in the market to this farmer, son of Citrane—all thanks to you! Take me! I will abase myself. I will be no trouble, make no trouble, not even speak to this wench of yours you seem so keen on. All I ask—"

At these words, Bellamia kicked her horse forward and struck out at Aster with a stick. "Get out of our way, you little trouble-maker! You can die here better than 'flict yourself on us!"

Aster took the blow on her raised forearm. She screamed and waved her arms about over her head. Fremant restrained Bellamia, saying to Aster, "You have no claim on me. I regret the wrong I did you, but this is a military expedition. You can't come with us."

As if to reinforce his words, Essanits shouted to them not to fall behind.

When Fremant put spur to flank, Aster seized his leg and began screaming as she ran, half-dragged, beside him. He tried to shake her off, eventually striking her on the side of her head. She fell away. Staggering backward, she fell and lay on the ground, crying and calling. Bellamia, departing from the scene, raised a finger at her.

The cortege reached the brow of the incline, then crossed over it, out of Aster's sight.

They rode through the day, stopping only once to eat unleavened bread and a sliver of insect meat. They were now in wilder country, where the endeavors of mankind did not prevail. At sunset they made camp. They sat around a small fire to eat, but had little to say—except, of course, for Essanits, who spoke gravely of God's plan, which had surely conveyed them across light-years of space to spread his word on Stygia. Nobody agreed with him, nobody disagreed.

Fremant and Bellamia slept together that night nearby the

others, although he had not forgotten his earlier habit of climbing a tree for safety during the hours of darkness. He lay against her generous sleeping body, staring up at the sky, where the six Brothers hastened by, one chasing the other. Shadows faintly followed them on the ground. In his mind were other shadows, as he reflected on his treatment of Aster.

As if disturbed in her sleep by his troubled thoughts, Bellamia awoke and sighed voluptuously.

"Are you all right?"

"Yes. Just thinking things over."

Snuggling against him, she gazed up at the great canopy of stars glistening in impressive disorder overhead.

"Where's Earth?" she asked. "The solar system?"

"No one knows. Somewhere up there . . ."

"And did God own the Earth?"

"It's just a legend. God or the Devil . . ."

DAYS FOLLOWED during which they progressed steadily. For two days they made their way through a sparse forest where the trees were scarcely taller than they. Every tree seemed to present a remarkable uniformity, each with only a certain number of branches, even a certain number of leaves, in a sinister form of duplication. Those trees, as they passed, immediately turned their leaves from green to yellow to brown, as if offended by the trekkers; so that they inadvertently left behind them a trail of dead leaves.

The forest fell away. For three more days they traveled, and for part of the time followed a shallow river in which the men wallowed and the horses drank. The landscape here was empty of foliage and broken, while mountains loomed ahead. Moving farther, they found salack growing in a clump on the riverbank; farther on, the herb spread over the stony banks. A little farther still, the river plunged over a cliff.

Bellamia was the first to pluck some of the leaves and begin chewing.

"Lovely! Lovely! Extra strong!" she exclaimed. Soon all were chewing it. At first, it had a positive effect on their mood.

"Ah, I could ride right up that mountain and then some!" shouted Tragonn, standing up in his stirrups, and a minute later he had tumbled off his mount.

"How fortunate we are to be here where Jesus once trod!" cried Essanits, sitting in the midst of a green patch and letting his horse wander. "He found no humans here and so he left. But this blessed herb he left behind for us, to cheer us on our way!"

"There's Jesus!" cried Wellmod, pointing. "Come join us! Jesus, yoo-hoo!"

None of the others could see Jesus.

They heard the sound of a waterfall. Following the river, they came to the edge of an immense cliff. It seemed to their distorted senses that at this point Jesus or someone as strong as Jesus had taken a mighty ax and cleaved the world in two. The water fell in an arc, plunging down into the gulf below. It was impossible to see how far it fell, for the great cloud of spray arising concealed everything below it. A rainbow played amid the cloud of countless water drops.

Fremant and Bellamia lay on the edge of the cliff, staring down, amazed at the grandeur of the sight. They chewed as they stared, as moisture scattered up to wet their faces.

Tragonn and Klarnort had also chewed quantities of the

herb, not bothering even to gather it, eating it where it grew, faces close to the ground. Suddenly as one, they jumped to their feet and sprang into the saddles of their horses.

Lashing the poor brutes on, they galloped toward the fall, shouting, "Jesus, man! We're coming! Coming!"

To the brink they drove, almost trampling Bellamia, never hesitating, on, on, leaping into the great gulf, to fall together with the falling waters.

Fremant watched it all in shock. Men and animals were digested into the all-enveloping mist, never to be seen again. The rainbow effect flickered, the great endless orgasm of water never faltered.

Sick with horror, he staggered to his feet.

"You and your stupid talk of Jesus!" he bellowed at their leader.

Bellamia tried to hush him. "I have known this stuff, so I'm immune, but these others . . ."

Essanits made no answer.

"It is God's will" was all he uttered, pronouncing the words in thick tones.

"It's nothing of the sort! Why didn't you stop them?"

For answer, Essanits swung an arm over his head in a gesture commanding them to move on. At his third attempt, he managed to haul himself into the saddle and kick Hengriss to action.

THE GASH IN THE WORLD marked a change in the landscape. Plains and lowlands were left behind. The way became steeper and more broken. Crumbling cliffs arose. Vegetation, sparse at the best of times, became even rarer. They traveled over regolith. The hooves of the horses stirred up dust, even as their sounds echoed against the rock face. The cliffs closed in on either side. Heat climbed with altitude. Rider became more separated from rider. Wellmod and his livestock fell far behind the rest of the group. Fremant found his thoughts transfixed by the terrible afterimage of the two men on their horses, galloping into the gulf to their death.

Eventually, Essanits called a halt by a place where collapsing rock had created a spacious cave. It was early afternoon. He sat on the dark, enduring Hengriss, looking back down the trail, with Chankey beside him.

As the others came slowly up, Essanits directed them to tether their horses against the rock, where long grass grew, then to go into the cave.

"Ha, Dimoff's due," said Bellamia.

"So Chankey informs me," said Essanits. "We will weather it here." He shouted to Wellmod as the lad arrived that he should tie up the packhorses with the other horses and drive the goats into the cave. So they all assembled, rather uncomfortably.

Bellamia and Chankey started a fire from pieces of deadwood. Soon, she was smoking the place out as she prepared a meal. Essanits settled down uncomplainingly, closing his eyes without relaxing his stern expression.

When Fremant came in from watering the horses, Bellamia told him to stake a place for them at the rear of the cave. He looked into the uninviting dark, scarcely illuminated by the fire's glow.

"We don't know what may be back there."

"Don't be cowardly. Cold will enter with the coming of the Shawl. It's warmer at the back."

Reluctantly, he did as he was bid. She joined him when they had eaten their meal.

"I'm hot now, Free. Feel me! Someone has left an old sack here. It's comfortable to rest yourself against."

"A sack? No one has been here before."

"How about Essanits?" She lowered her voice. "He may have come this way on his killing expedition, before he found God or Jesus."

Fremant felt behind him. There was certainly a plump thing, like a well-stuffed bag, lying at their backs, covered by fur. He prodded it, afraid it might somehow be alive, but there was no movement in response.

It was still golden afternoon. The heat shimmered in the canyon. But in the eastern sky, already the Shawl began to spread its folds. Chankey left the cave to stare up at it, and crossed himself.

Wellmod, speaking to no one in particular, asked, "Did Jesus put the Shawl up there, do you think?"

"Maybe he did," Essanits said. "If he found the Dogovers were not behaving as he had hoped."

"What about us, then? We're behaving nicely, aren't we? Why don't he cancel it?"

Essanits made no response.

Gradually, the day became overcast. The great black mass of dust and debris poured between Stygia and the Sun. A chill shadow soon prevailed, turning rapidly into cold night. All felt impressed and oppressed by the eclipse. They huddled together in silence, while the goats bleated in dismay.

Essanits spoke from the darkness. "We will sleep as much as

possible for the next two days, sleep and rest. Bellamia, see that the goats provide us with sufficient milk."

"They can't yield if they can't feed, can they now?"

"Do your best."

A long silence ensued before Essanits spoke again. "I shall take this opportunity to make you all better informed. While I am an intellectual, as you are not, I still believe you will find knowledge helpful, not least because we are on the quest for an alien race.

"Once the tyrant Astaroth was overthrown, we found in his quarters many records taken from the ship—which you recall was named *New Worlds*. These records make clear the sorry state of affairs on Earth which led to the development and launch of the ship.

"The section of the world known as 'Thewest' was the most technologically advanced region, and had been for several centuries. There, the population lived well on the whole. They had hygiene in their homes, food on their shelves, and freedom to believe what they would. Science and the arts were respected—or, at worst, paid lip service. It was the most desirable part of the world in which to live.

"One of the things that made it desirable was that the soils were, in general, good—unlike on this planet—and that the inhabitants had learned the processes of irrigation and good husbandry, here unknown, or impossible . . .

"There were, however, other regions besides Thewest. They—in reaction against or imitation of Thewest—slowly gained power. In the East was a great and remarkable civilization, its roots established many centuries before those of the nations making up Thewest. It had frequently suffered disruptions but was not warlike and, in its increasing prosperity, became more like Thewest, espousing many Western values. Its peoples were intelligent, its social systems orderly.

"A third sector lay between these two sectors, the East and Thewest. This sector had deep divisions within it and was, on the whole, ruled by despots, ruined by corruption. Hunger, the subjugation of women, torture, disease—all these were commonplace. A religion which once had elements of benevolence became twisted into a creed of vengeance and hatred—its malevolence aimed in the main against Thewest. With its extreme poverty went extreme wealth for a very few. These elements, together combined with ruthlessness, mounted an effective onslaught against Thewest—Brothers above!" he exclaimed.

His monologue had been violently interrupted.

At the back of the cave, a large, black, furry thing had suddenly roused itself from a form of catalepsy and was trying to make its way toward the cave mouth, blundering first into Fremant and then Essanits as it hurried to get out. The goats were plunged into a frenzy.

Chankey snatched up a brand from the fire and rushed up to attack the thing. The thing in its haste had struck the cliff wall opposite and tumbled momentarily to the ground. Chankey was upon it, his knife slashing.

"Spare the poor creature," ordered Essanits. "It did us no harm."

"I'll do *it* harm! Scared the shittle outta me!"

The creature was dying under the blade, oozing a thick liquid which stank of something like butyric acid, the compound which makes human vomit smell disgusting.

Recovering from their startlement, the trekkers came out to gaze at the thing as it lay twitching.

Its body was segmented in six parts, each part sprouting two rather feeble-looking legs, now waving their last. Fine hair covered its every part, except for the last segment, which did duty as a face. Here, four multisegmented eyes were situated. They gleamed in the torchlight with iridescent colors, continuing to gleam so after the creature finally gave up its last struggle for life.

"No mouth!" Fremant exclaimed.

"It must be a what-you-call-it? You know . . ." Bellamia struggled for words. "Not sort of like a—what? The final form."

"You mean a larval stage," said Essanits coldly. At which point he was sent staggering by another of the same species emerging from the cave mouth, and then another. Both made a great whirring noise, as their supposed legs became small wings which propelled them into the air. Luckier than the creature which had preceded them, they did not run into the cliff face. Instead, they circled, still whirring and terrifying the tethered horses, and were away into the dark sky.

Wellmod clung to Fremant's arm. "I ain't going back in there!"

"Hang on and we'll see if any more come out. They must, um, hibernate until Dimoff comes. It's a signal for them to— well, I don't know—maybe to change . . ."

"Well, they appear to be harmless," said Essanits.

"Except for the filthy stink," said Chankey. His brand was burning low. They stood there in the darkness, undecided. Wellmod went to calm the horses. Nothing else emerged from the cave, and so they cautiously returned to its shelter and stoked up the fire.

"I WILL CONTINUE with what I was telling you," said Essanits, when they had settled down. "Listen carefully. There are lessons to be learned.

"Thewest in its heyday had enjoyed a policy of laissez-faire. Many people from other parts of the world were welcomed within its borders, to make what they could of a better way of life. This eventually created a weakness within the social structure, so that unison was broken, freedoms curtailed, dissent stifled. Deathwatch beetles bored into the very beams of the culture.

"Many of those from the Middle sector were peaceable. Some, however, were hostile to the Christy-earn culture of Thewest. As they became better organized—using the very communicatium tools devised by Thewest—they inflicted much damage on the structures of Thewest. As the infrastructures were weakened, so the governments became more restrictive—in some cases more tyrannical. Thus the terrorists were achieving their end. Of course, Thewest had its own faults. It made the mistake of invading some territories of the enemy. Gradually, year by year, it was weakened."

The audience in the cave listened with varying degrees of disinterest compounded by incomprehension.

"The massive *New Worlds* was constructed in a last-ditch attempt to save the values of Thewest. Volunteers were carefully vetted before being deconstructed and inserted into the computerized entails of the ship.

"The very day after the capital city of Thewest was destroyed by a hydrogen bomb, *New Worlds* was launched on its predetermined course for this distant world we call Stygia. The determination was that this great scientific feat was something no endeavor by the relatively hidebound terrorist nations could emulate. Western values would be safe on Stygia."

Silence fell, reinforcing the darkness and isolation of their situation.

"What about Astaroth?" Fremant asked at last. "Had he got Western values?"

After a pause, Essanits said that Astaroth was "austere"—a good Western value. Unfortunately it had included negative values, too, like an obsessive love of power.

No one said anything more.

As he lay in the darkness, he thought, *I am Paul Fadhil Abbas Ali. Why am I not happy?*

The cold, the artificial night, became more intense.

SIX

A VOICE ASKED FREMANT, "Why did you write what you did?"

He replied that it was only one line. The line about the PM.

"One line can be a fucking signal, can't it?"

"Not in this case . . . You promised to let me go free."

"There's been an incident. Which prime minister were you referring to in this crap book of yours? The present one?"

"No actual prime minister."

"But you knew it would be an invitation to terrorists to kill the sitting prime minister?"

"I knew no such thing."

"How did your wife get involved in all this?"

"All what?"

"ALL THIS, YOU CUNT!"

"She wasn't involved."

"You are fucking lying as usual, you fucking little creep. She married you, didn't she?"

"No. I mean, yes, we were married but she never wrote a word of my book."

"Yeah? She corrected your grammar, di'n' she?"

"Yes." The blow on the side of his jaw knocked him off the stool he was perched on. He sprawled on the floor, thinking he could never move again.

"Get up, you bastard. Don't just lay there."

He got up. The interrogation continued.

It continued for another hour. Afterward, he was thrown into darkness, where he lay in pain. The cockroach visited him. The flies buzzed about his ears.

He thought, *I am who I am. Why am I not miserable? Why do I feel so little?*

His feelings were muddied and unclear. At least he knew he now hated the British, the nation he had once greatly admired. His uncle, who had been a lawyer in his Uganda days, had read much English literature, with a particular affection for such works as De Quincey's *Confessions of an English Opium Eater*, with its masterly and elaborate prose, and the learned and abstruse *Anatomy of Melancholy* by Robert Burton.

At night, when the family gathered for the evening meal, his uncle would tell them of these books, sometimes reading aloud the beautiful prose.

Some such books had accompanied his father on his escape to England and formed his own early reading matter. Only later did he realize that he had learned of an impoverished yet dignified England which had passed away. A wave of materialism had overtaken England. A disgraceful hedonism was all, a hedonism often taking the form of riots at football matches, binge-drinking and street violence, vomiting and urinating on pavements, sporadic racism. There was no—or next to no—spiritual life remaining. *The Decline and Fall of the Roman Empire* was being repeated—in a minor key . . .

It was for spiritual life he yearned. He longed to leave the sordid England that had imprisoned him. But where to go for refuge? The U.S.A.? Too formidable . . . Certainly not to the Middle East, where a mental stasis, reinforced by the rigid tenets of the Koran, prevailed. Not to one of those hidebound little hamlets in Saudi Arabia or Iraq, for sure . . . There was Indonesia, with its dread military regime. There was Malaysia, where matters were relatively benign—but otherwise so foreign to his timid nature. India? Too confusing. China? But the China he admired had transformed itself into a giant, while England had dwindled. He longed for somewhere distant.

Light-years away . . .

WHEN THE TWO-DAY DARKNESS CLEARED, when the scattered blackness of the Shawl tailed off to the west, the trekkers came out of their cave and killed one of the goats, which they roasted over a spit. The horses had eaten all the grass by the cliffside and needed attention. So the men and Bellamia set off again, still chewing the stringy goat meat. Essanits led them, riding on black Hengriss.

For two days and nights they traveled among the wearying mazes of rock. At last they came to a place where comparatively lush pastures beckoned, where no more than the odd rock stood sentinel, as if a monument to something dead. The ground undulated like frozen waves. Here the silence was unbroken, except for scufflings in the grass where many unevolved insects found their home.

While they allowed the horses to graze, they looked about them. The grass gave out ahead, leaving only barren earth and stones. They could see a great distance, where cumulus cloud was piled on the horizon.

"What a dump!" said Chankey. He spat.

"Not too far now," said Essanits encouragingly. "Be of good cheer, lads."

As he spoke, Wellmod pointed ahead, gasping.

They looked. They stared.

At a distance from them, something resembling a great sail appeared, moving close to the horizon. This enormous triangular fin was adorned with many colors, colors not bright but subdued, the edge of each color merging fuzzily into the next, so that their diversity created a unity. A pattern was formed, centering near the peak of the sail into an oval target vaguely resembling an eye.

The sail moved majestically, its colors seeming to change slowly as it went. Something in its magnificence left the humans speechless. It was the very essence of unimpeachable beauty.

Fremant's mind filled with images of sensuality. He recalled fleetingly that he had lain naked with a beautiful pale woman with fair hair. A name came back to him in a whisper—Doris. Then it was gone, such that he could not recall it, and a stifling sense of loss descended on him.

"So so bewful!" exclaimed Bellamia, nearby.

"What can it be?" asked Wellmod in a whisper.

"A vision . . ."

The sail began to move behind a distant concealing mound. Less and less of it remained visible. Still they stared. Soon only the oblong eye remained, seeming to gaze back at them from the horizon. Then it, too, was gone. For a while they did not speak.

They looked to Essanits for explanation.

"I can only guess . . . Fremant, have you seen such a thing before?"

"Never."

"I can only guess that it was a wing of something."

"Then, could be it was the wing of the black things from the cave? Their next stage of development . . ."

For all their talk, the immense supposed wing remained a mystery to them.

"Better get moving," said Chankey, sighing deeply. They had all seen something which represented what they lacked.

ON THE FOLLOWING DAY, they came to a great body of water. Reeds fringed its edges, between which the element glittered, reflecting the sun as from a mirror. It was a lake that appeared almost as vast as an inland sea. The waters were still, as if waiting. Fremant recalled his previous alarming experience in a body of water, from which the thing grappled with him.

Essanits pointed to the distant bank, where they could make out a grove of trees.

"That's our destination. There lies Incessible."

"But how do we get across this bluggerating lake?"

"The water is not deep. The horses will carry us across."

"Supposing there is something in the water that will attack us?"

"I don't think so."

The sun shone as they stood there indecisively. They were reluctant to enter the water.

Fremant asked what they would do if they found some surviving Dogovers on the far side of the lake. Essanits fixed a glare of burning dislike on him. He replied flatly that they would take any survivors back to Stygia City, and restore them there, should they wish to return. If they did not wish to return, then there would be a ceremony to mark human penitence for the wrong that had been done.

Will they understand that?

Will they not rise up and kill us?

Will they commit group suicide, as the humans had witnessed before?

Essanits shrugged. They must trust in God and hope for the best.

Bellamia asked how they could understand a foreign tongue. She said that she would cook them a meal. It might prove more effective in the way of communication than a ceremony. Food was the universal language, she said.

Essanits gave a grudging assent.

Wellmod said that the Dogovers might kill *them*.

Fremant thought, If I die, on the morrow I shall wake in Paradise . . .

Chankey goaded his mount into the flood.

One by one, the others followed.

THE LAKE WATER WAS COLD, and yet shallow, as Essanits had said. The horses struggled forward. After one hour, they were still not halfway across the lake. After two hours, when the horses were visibly tiring, they appeared to be closing in on the far shore.

Chankey said, "There's something in the water by us, following us. Keep your guns ready."

Bellamia and Fremant had already seen a telltale line of ripple on either side of them. Bellamia became very nervous. She tried to spur her horse on, but the animal was too weary to respond. They were all anxious and tense.

Wellmod suddenly gave a cry. A pair of giant mandibles, black in color, flashing in the sunlight, rose from the water. They surfaced from beside Wellmod, who was bringing up the rear, as usual. But the creature was not attacking him. Rather, the huge jaws closed over the last of the string of goats. The goat struggled but, within a few seconds, was dragged below. A great splashing ensued, lasting until a whitish pulp floated up, bubbling, to the surface. Wellmod's yells of horror vied with the cries of the horses. Essanits quickly brought his horse under control. Chankey's mount plunged and reared. Chankey, less of a horseman than his leader, was thrown into the water.

He was at once seized by one of the underwater creatures. He rose, spluttering, one raised arm and his neck caught in a pair of the hornlike mandibles. He managed to bring the trapped arm around so that he could grasp one of the threatening jaws; with his other hand he took hold of the other jaw. In his struggle to wrench the two mandibles apart, he dragged his attacker half out of the water. What appeared was something less stag-beetle-like than spider-like, with a balloon body studded with eyes and trailing hairy legs—a monstrous compound of a gigantic insect, gray and beige and blue. Then this tawdry thing dived, and Chankey was pulled under. He rose again, bent backward, face red with agony and exertion. With one desperate heave, he tore the mandibles apart. A yellowish puslike substance spewed out about the waters around him.

Gasping, Chankey hauled himself back on his horse. He lay across its back, gasping.

The water was immediately beaten into a froth. Several pairs of the black horns appeared, then disappeared, as the submerged horrors fought to devour the remains of the broken monster.

Essanits called to everyone to make what haste they could away from the scene. Badly shaken, they pressed on, to gain the shore a few minutes later.

They rode into a sheltering grove of trees well above the waterline, to throw themselves down, exhausted, on the ground. The horses, too, collapsed.

"Are you all right, Chankey?" Bellamia and Fremant went over to him. Chankey was doubled up, his arms clutching each other, his knees near his chin. He rocked back and forth in pain.

"That bastard thing nearly got me. Jupers! Something stung me. But I'm all right . . ."

Staring up at the foliage above them, Bellamia, sighing, said, "Dreadful! This world where insects predommy—predom— have the upper hand."

Fremant's response was to ask if a world where men had the upper hand was much better.

No one made any response to that. He lay there, exhausted. Bellamia propped herself beside him, stroking his wet hair, smoothing his brow, whispering endearments, without a thought for herself.

His heart and mind were filled with love for her as if with a newly opened flower.

Getting to his knees, Essanits began to pray aloud. He stressed his own sinfulness, and that of all men. He claimed that the beautiful sail they had seen was a sign from the Almighty, a promise of redemption. He hoped that they would find forgiveness if they rescued the remnant of the autochthonous race. He begged for their safe deliverance back to Stygia City.

On all these matters he elaborated greatly.

"Oh, for Joe's sake, do shut up!" said Chankey. "I can't stand any more of this stuff."

"I'm praying to save your soul," said Essanits sternly.

"I just want to ask," said Fremant, when a loud amen had been pronounced—"if Jesus walked this planet once on a time, did he walk as a man or as an insect?"

"That's a most irreligious question."

"No. I'm curious. A man or an insect?"

It was Wellmod who jumped in with an answer. "'Course he walked as a man. He didn't walk as a lion or a tiger on Earth, did he?"

"That's why animals don't go to Heaven, I guess," Chankey replied. He began coughing violently.

Essanits stood up and ordered them to be on their way.

Fremant helped Chankey to his feet. They picked their way through the trees, climbing the slope as they went.

At the crest of the slope, where the trees gave out, they stood and surveyed a narrow valley. In the valley stood a number of leather tents. Each tent rose to a point and was decorated with colored images. Fremant had seen a similar tent previously.

"We're here," Essanits said. "This is the place." They dismounted, tying their horses and the remaining goats to trees.

"Chankey, you and I will go down on foot and speak to them. Fremant, you and Wellmod and the woman will remain up here. Stay alert in case of trouble."

" 'The woman' could kick your aggorant ass," said Bellamia quietly, as the two men set off.

The tents looked dilapidated. Only one appeared properly maintained. From it emerged a two-legged creature and a dog. They stood defensively, regarding the approaching men.

A white shelf materialized between the two parties. It seemed to stretch the length of the valley. It floated approximately knee-high. Its surface became stippled with small shapes, many of them round, all dun-colored. For part of the time it was transparent.

"It's their speech!" Fremant called to Essanits. "They're trying to communicate!"

Essanits and Chankey had halted in puzzlement before the manifestation. They made no attempt at a response. The shelf changed to a reddish color.

Chankey gave a roar of anger. He rushed forward, through the illusory shelf, toward the Dogover and the dog.

"Careful!" shouted Essanits, as he, too, ran forward. The dog leaped out of the way. The Dogover snatched up a pole, pointing it so adroitly that Chankey ran into it, being struck full in the chest. His charge carried him on. He ran into the small Dogover. They fell together on the ground. Chankey head-butted the other. The Dogover fell back, hitting his head on one of the many stones.

Essanits arrived, to haul Chankey off his opponent. "I'm stung," said Chankey, in a choking voice.

"You soul-damned fool!"

Fremant had run down and seized the dog, who seemed to

be focused on his prone friend. A minute later, Bellamia came with a wicker cage which one of the packhorses had been carrying. Between them, they crammed the dog into the cage and closed the door.

The Dogover rose up groggily from the ground into a sitting position.

"Are you all right?" said Essanits, kneeling, steadying the little person by an arm.

The little person muttered something, closed his eyes—and died.

"Oh God! Chankey, you violent fool," Essanits exclaimed. "You have killed the last living Dogover."

"No, no, 'course I haven't. Not on your life, not on anyone's life. We just got to look in these other tents. They're full of 'em. Miserable little critters. They're pimghees."

"You mean pygmies. Stay here! The rest of you search these tents. Go careful."

But Chankey was off at a rolling trot, running unsteadily. He had almost reached one of the more dilapidated tents when he fell. He rolled on the ground, cursing, tearing at his shirt. Then he lay still until the others reached him.

Bellamia knelt beside him, felt his wrist for a pulse. There was none. In his agonies, Chankey had bared his stomach. Noticing, Bellamia recoiled in horror. A large strawberry blister had formed just below his navel. Below its surface she saw small white things like maggots, swimming.

Speechlessly, she indicated the blister to the others.

Chankey had indeed been stung, as he claimed. In the time he had been in the waters of the lake, in the grip of the beetle-like monster, it had planted its seed below his skin.

Fremant and Wellmod shivered with disgust.

"We must give him burial," said Essanits. "And bury these loathsome insects with him."

"How can we dig a grave?" Fremant asked. "We don't know what may be lurking in these other tents. At least we've got this dog. Let's go home. This whole expedition has been a disaster. We should have waited for another push-pull and flown here."

Essanits glared at him. "I frankly have no liking for you, Fremant. It shocks me that you should think of leaving this poor fellow unburied, to rot here on unhallowed ground."

"Why is it better to bury him in 'unhallowed ground'? Besides, he has ruined your plans, hasn't he? Killing off the last surviving Dogover!"

"We must be forgiving in the face of death."

In the end, after much argument, they laid Chankey's body across one of the horses and rode back to the lake. There they tied a stone to one of his legs and sank him in the chilly waters. Essanits said a solemn prayer for his soul, while the thing in the water caroused on his corpse.

SEVEN

THE LONG JOURNEY BACK to Haven was marked by the further deterioration of the relationship between Fremant and Essanits. Fremant protested that it was useless and cruel to keep the Dogover's dog in the cage.

"We are taking the creature to Stygia City. Safelkty has perfected the Cereb machine in the *New Worlds* laboratories. That will allow us to read the dog's mind, which should retain some recorded images of the past culture. It's our duty."

"What's the dog likely to say? 'Down, boy'? 'Fetch'? It's a waste of time. You're just hoping to save face . . ."

"Nonsense. The dog could prove valuable."

Fremant closed his eyes, raising a hand in rejection. "Think, will you? Ever since we landed on Stygia, our efforts have been devoted to the genocide of the Dogovers. Weren't you the leader of that? We've just killed off the last one between us, and you think this wretched dog 'could prove valuable.' What kind of a fool are you?"

"Who are you to challenge me? The day will come when we see that it was necessary to destroy the autochthonous race in order to establish God's will on the planet."

"Really? Then I don't think much of your God."

Bellamia caught his wrist. "Don't anger him, Free!" she said. It was unclear whether she meant God or Essanits.

They journeyed on, becoming ever more hungry. The rest of their goats had been seized by the monsters on their return through the lake. Wellmod suggested they eat the dog, but the men said no.

The dog lay supine, almost inert, although its eyes were open and alert. It only vaguely resembled any breed of terrestrial dog, although much of its insect origin had been shed. Its body was segmented in four sections, the hind three of which bore pairs of stiltlike legs. Small tubes with lidded ends projected from each section, to carry air into the body. Lungs had yet to develop on Stygia.

Its tail folded neatly over the ridge of its back when not in use. A tassel at the end of the tail proved on inspection to be six delicate fingers. When Fremant offered the dog crumbs of bread, the tail would protrude through the bars of its cage and the fingers, taking hold of the crumbs, would convey them daintily to its mouth.

Its head carried the sharp-jawed mouth of its kind, and two large eyes. There appeared to be no ears. With no auditory function, the dog projected imagery instead. This it evidently refused to do while in captivity.

They saw the great sail again. It floated grandly on a gentle wind. They stopped on the trail to stare. It was so unlikely, so beautiful: the very image of serenity. On this occasion there were two sails, flying close together. When the wind direction changed, the twin sails began to head toward the travelers.

Both sails bore their harmoniously tinted markings. One set of markings was brighter than its mate's.

"That'll be the female," said Bellamia.

"The male, more likely," said Essanits.

As the sails approached—gradually, magnificently—the group sought defensive positions behind a rock barrier. They were now able to judge the immense size of the sails, and to see that a curved stanchion ran from the base of the leading edge to the top of the sail, becoming more slender as it rose, to hold the sail steady. The sail itself appeared almost paper thin, delicate as a moth's wing.

Both sails were drawing near now, drifting only a few feet aboveground.

Glorious as the sails were, the body below them, from which they grew, was another matter: a snakelike legged insect, gray of body, equipped with massive jaws in front and something resembling a stinger at its rear.

Still the sails came nearer. Essanits raised his gun, steadied it on his left arm, and fired. The bullet hit the front end of the flier, which burst, showering the leader with a stinking, greenish pus.

For a moment, the sail sailed on. Then it faltered, declined, the body hit a rock, and the entire grand structure slowly sank to the ground. The other sail never paused, but floated forward on the wind, finally to disappear into the blue distance.

Bellamia and Fremant pulled up handfuls of grass to mop each other down from the splashes of pus. Essanits went over with a swagger to inspect his target.

"There you are!" he said. "Something to eat now."

"Bluggeration! Who wants to eat *that* stinking thing?" Bellamia exclaimed. "But maybe if it were cooked . . ."

Fremant went to inspect the great sail. Already its colors were fading, the fabric crumpling like an old tissue. An intense melancholy overcame him, a sorrow he could hardly bear or understand.

Coming up behind him, Essanits said, "Stop moping, man, and let's get on."

Fremant swung around and struck him savagely in the chest.

WHEN AT LAST THEY ENTERED HAVEN, they found it much changed. Duplicates of a new flag flew everywhere. New wooden buildings were going up, and men—several of them in uniform—thronged the place, shouting and calling to one another in a stupidly military manner.

A group of resident women in dusty homespun robes looked on hopelessly; all seemed old and worn, although two of them held babies in their arms.

A new center had been created. A banner proclaimed it to be LOCAL GOVERNMENT, although it flew the flag of Stygia City. Essanits marched straight through its door as if he had thought of nothing else throughout the trek.

Bellamia and Fremant climbed their steps and went to wash. She fed the dog, who produced a swirl of red between them, possibly a kind of flower. She took it as thanks.

"You're a good doggie, ugly as you are." And in an aside to Fremant, "Another bluggy type of insect, too."

After a brief meal, Fremant went to see Utrersin to find out what was happening. The man was working, as usual, in his forge.

"I never thought I'd see you again," he said, without a smile, setting down his hammer. "This dump is now like an anthill— full of newcomers, all talking about freedom. You might think that was okay by me. You ain't got no notion how orders for guns is increasted, but me, I'm agin such change."

"What's going on, then?"

He straightened himself, pushing his hair back from his damp forehead. The hair flopped back as usual. "I ain't the only one what's got more work. There's men flatt'ning out ground so's push-pulls can land here. There's men building a road or a railway or sommat from here to Stig City. There's men training up for a sort of local militia. You wouldn't know the place. No peace now."

"Sounds like improvements to me."

He looked through his overhanging hair with a grin. "You always was a bit soft in the head, ole feller."

As he was trudging back across the square, Fremant was stopped by two powerful men wearing uniform caps. "You are wanted for a meeting in the government offices."

"Why's that?"

"You was on the trek with Gov'ner Essanits, wasn't you?"

"Governor, is he now?"

"He's gov'ner of somewhere or other," said the leader of the two men indifferently. "Come on, get a move on. You don't want trouble, do you?"

He went with them, not without misgivings.

No sooner had the three of them passed through the door of the local government office than he was seized. He kicked and struggled, but the two men caught his head in a lock and were almost choking him. He was pushed into a small cell with wooden walls. He smelled the scent of fresh-cut wood. Furiously, he hammered on the door.

The only light in the dark cell filtered through a gap under the door. No response came to his hammering. He gave up and went to sit down, defeated, on a narrow ledge which served as a bench.

Time dawdled. A sheet of paper was passed under the door. He picked it up, squinting to make out the text in the dim light. In elaborate lettering, it read:

> By Command of the Government of Haven City, you are imprisoned pending trial for the act of striking the Governor of Seldonia, as the region between Haven City and Stygia City is now known. Such ruffianism is no longer legal under new state laws. The date of your trial will be announced shortly. Meantime, you are instructed to keep quiet or food and drink will be withheld.

It was signed: "The Mayor of Haven City."

He flung the paper down in exasperation.

He stayed awake as long as possible. Eventually, he sat on the ground with his back to a wooden wall, drew up his knees, and slumped into a deep sleep.

A ROARING IN HIS EYES, a sound like tumultuous applause, a feeling he was falling, endlessly, through a medium that was space and yet not space.

A woman was withdrawing a hypodermic needle from his left arm. A portable lamp stood on a nearby trolley.

"That's better," she said. She had brown eyes behind rimless glasses. Her expression was not unkindly. "How do you feel? You don't look too good. I'll get you a glass of water in a moment."

He could say nothing. He was glad to hear a woman's voice.

She busied herself with the trolley she had wheeled into the room. He knew the room. To his distorted senses it was vast. It had once possessed grandeur. There were marble cherubs by the fireplace, decorated alcoves and ceiling, a domed ceiling, and floral wallpaper, now peeling from the walls.

The woman turned back to him and, seeing he was more alert, remarked that he must have walked into a door, since he had a badly bruised left eye.

He managed to speak. "I have bruises all over."

"There, there!" She came and loomed over him, looking sympathetic. "Many prisoners harm themselves. It's a guilt reaction to confinement." ·

He did not attempt to contradict her. Indeed, he was almost overcome with emotion to hear a sympathetic voice, to see a sympathetic expression in this place of suffering.

"What's happened to Bellamia? She should have a proper funeral." Seeing the woman's look of puzzlement, he corrected himself and said that he meant Doris.

"Oh yes, Doris. Of course. Of course." She wagged a finger at him. "I want you to sign a document. Then the glass of water."

As she turned back to her trolley, he saw she was a thickset woman, very broad in the hips and buttocks. She wore a heavy cloth jacket and skirt, much like a uniform. Such liking as he had initially felt faded at the sight of that formidable rear view.

"Am I going to be given my freedom?"

Without turning around, she said, "You are still claiming you are innocent, eh?"

"I am. I *am* innocent. Completely innocent. I'm a British citizen." He added, "In fact, I am a good deal more innocent than many another British citizen."

She turned to him, her face suddenly grim. Her hair was cut short and dyed blond. He caught a glimpse of its dark roots.

"But you're a Muslim. You made that remark about the British prime minister in your book . . ."

"It was just one joke among many."

She was unmoved. "Tell me another of these so-called jokes."

He sighed. "Well, for instance, there's a character called Snowy Snowden, he's a male nurse, and he goes into an Italian fish restaurant and orders a spina bifida . . ."

Not a muscle in her face moved.

She asked where he was when he was arrested.

"I had been playing cricket. They came and arrested me in the pavilion."

"Playing *cricket*?"

"Why not?"

"Was it some kind of alibi?"

"An alibi? What for? I had done nothing wrong—beyond scoring only a miserable nine runs for my side."

The woman had a way of not hearing what he said. Putting on a sympathetic expression again, she wedged one of her hips against the ledge on which he was sprawling and said, "Well, you'll be free to go now. You'll get your watch and the contents of your pockets back, of course. We hope your stay here has not been too uncomfortable."

"Where am I? What country are we in?"

"You have to sign this document first." She handed it to him. He squinted at it with his good eye.

The document, with various flourishes, stated that the interrogations had all been fair and conducted in accordance with the precepts of British justice, and within the limitations imposed by the Geneva Conventions, that he had been well treated during his stay, that he had not sustained any injuries, that he had been well fed. That all his properties had been returned to him, including his British passport. That he was not being charged for the use of his room.

"This is absolute bullshit!"

"You refuse to sign it?"

"There's no mention of my wife, Doris. What has happened to her body?"

She brought out a mobile phone and tapped at it. She looked hard at its rectangular face.

"You are Fadhil Abbas Ali?"

"Paul Fadhil Abbas Ali."

"There's no record that you have, or had, a wife. No mention of any Doris. Just sign the document, will you? Don't fuck about. I haven't got all day."

"But I must know about my wife. Surely you can understand that?"

Suddenly, she was furious. "Sign the fucking document, will you? Else, you'll be banged up in here till you rot."

For answer, he tore the document in two.

The woman brought up a brawny fist and struck him on his bad left eye.

HE ROUSED SLOWLY, his brain numb, stiff with cold. His knees felt locked. Slowly, he straightened his legs. Cautiously, he stood up, a hand on the wooden wall for balance. His eye was hurting him.

There was nothing to be done but stand there.

The door was eventually unlocked. A man pushed it open and came in with a small tray. Another man stood guard just beyond the door.

"Here's your meal. Your trial will be coming up later today." Said as the man balanced the tray on the ledge.

"When? Morning or afternoon?"

"We'll have to see." He retreated, walking the few steps backward. The door was closed and locked after him.

The meal consisted of a crust of bread and an egg, and a small glass of water. He smelled the water cautiously before drinking.

Much later, the two guards who had arrested him came and took him to a small room at the rear of the building. "Don't worry," one of them said. "He's a pretty good guy."

There at a table sat Essanits. Two young secretaries sat at a table behind him. The guards came to attention and remained one on either side of Fremant. Through a window behind Essanits, he could see green things growing.

Essanits contemplated his prisoner for a while without speaking, his large, wide face expressionless. He was wearing a new white uniform.

"Fremant, I want you to do me a service."

When Fremant made no response, Essanits said, "You are aware that striking a governor—in this case, myself—is illegal. I could have you severely punished. I hope that a night in that cozy little cell has sufficiently adjusted your attitude. How was your meal?"

"Adequate."

"Adequate? Good. Perhaps the best we could hope for under the circumstances. I wish you to do me a service. Accompanied by guards, you will take the dog we captured to Stygia City, to Governor Safelkty, explain the circumstances under which it was caught, and hand it over for inspection."

"Why me? Why not you?"

"I am busy here. We must establish proper organization. I am determined to put Haven City in working order. What happened to your eye? We need to arrest Elder Deselden and all his clique for blasphemy. Etcetera, etcetera."

Fremant was silent, thinking, before he spoke again. "If you went back to Stygia City, Safelkty would probably kill you, wouldn't he?"

Essanits banged a fist down on the table, "Confound it, man, I am offering you a chance, instead of a trial, at which you would probably be found guilty and punished.

"You know me for a lenient man. I am attempting to help you. I know you are a strangely neurotic fellow with associative identity disorder. Take this opportunity I offer you to get out of this town—you and that bluggerational dog!"

THEY NO LONGER had to walk or ride, as formerly. Instead, they caught a carriage, a broad-wheeler. For a charge of three stigs apiece, Fremant and Bellamia crammed into its seats with four other people. Several other carriages passed on the way. They traveled through the newly designated province of Seldonia without event. A push-pull flew by overhead. In a push-pull they could have arrived in five minutes at the destination which had once taken them through three Dimoffs to gain.

Bellamia kissed Fremant as they set off. He noted that she always unthinkingly held his head when kissing him, as if afraid he might move away. But her soft and ample lips were hard to resist.

He did indeed love her. He regretted greatly that he was unable to love her with all of his being—as he felt the situation demanded. So he was especially kind, and kept his arm about her ample waist as they traveled, she with the caged dog on her lap. The dog radiated little fugitive pictograms, where naked people danced, to be transposed into leaves and blossoms; or was it leaves and blossoms that transposed themselves into naked people? In any case, these were friendly if disconcerting gestures from their captive.

As THEY HAD ANTICIPATED, Stygia City had changed. At a well-defined boundary, their broad-wheeler was halted by a guard post. The passengers alighted and were directed to enter the post, one by one. There they were interrogated in an amiable way and had to give their names, their occupations, and where they came from, as well as a statement on their health.

All six passengers were passed and presented with tickets which identified them.

"Don't lose them," the clerk advised.

Fremant scrutinized his and Bellamia's tickets. They were newly, if badly, printed and bore a signature: "Lord Safelkty, President of Stygia."

"So now he's president of the whole jupissing planet!" exclaimed Fremant.

"Where does it say that?" Bellamia stared blankly at the ticket. He remembered that she could not read. One or two of the other passengers experienced the same problem.

They went into the city.

It was much busier than they remembered it to be. Men were moving about in teams. Stalls had been set up, mostly attended by women. Slogans had been nailed up everywhere. BE GOOD CITIZENS, one of them urged. CHILDREN ARE OUR FUTURE. BUILD MORE. LET WORK BE YOUR GOD.

The block previously known as the Center was now designated Government Offices. Across its portals hung this long exhortation: CITIZENS, LEARN TO READ! OBTAIN A FREE ALFABET BOOK INSIDE. BECOME CLEVER. BE CLEVER. WE PROGRESS OR DIE. WORK FOR A BETTER LIFE—FOR YOURSELVES, FOR YOUR FRIENDS, FOR YOUR NEIGHBERS. IN THE FUTURE LIES HAPPINESS—IF WE SUCCEED! It was signed: "Lord Safelkty, President of Stygia."

When Fremant had read this notice aloud, he and Bellamia looked glumly at each other. "I'm clever enough," she said. "I don't want to be any more clever—or not to please him . . ."

Unlike Bellamia, Fremant was inspired by these signs, feeling that someone was trying to improve people's lives. But these reflections he kept to himself.

They entered the building, where a doorman directed them to New Arrivals, a counter, behind which a smiling woman stood.

"We need to see the president."

The woman never ceased to smile. "You can make an appointment with me. There may be a two-week wait, I must warn you."

"We have to see him today, lady."

"That can't be done, I'm afraid."

Bellamia set the caged dog down on the counter. It projected a small white shelf. On the shelf there slowly emerged a bloody beaten head, the head of the Dogover killed beyond the lake. Maggots fell from its open mouth. The clerk lurched back in horror.

"I—I'll see what can be done. Please . . ."

A few minutes later they were entering the presidential suite. The waiting room was supervised by a man Fremant recognized as Hazelmarr, the youth who had stayed behind when they escaped from Astaroth's prison. Hazelmarr was no longer a youth. He had grown a thin mustache and cut off most of his hair. He wore heavy clothes. He was in a minor position of authority.

And in the widening of his eyes, and a slight stiffening, he showed he recognized Fremant.

"We have an appointment to speak to Safelkty," said Fremant, striding up to the desk.

"What's your business?" Hazelmarr inquired. "The president is occupied just now."

"I'm here on official business. I've come from Haven City. So announce me, will you?"

Hazelmarr's face remained expressionless. "You can't take that insect in with you."

He pointed with a pencil at the dog.

"This dog? I certainly can." He took the cage from Bellamia's hands and set it on the desk in front of Hazelmarr. The dog, startled, gave forth a series of brown and gray pentagons which rushed toward the clerk, fading only as they reached his face.

Hazelmarr gave a shriek. Lurching back, he tipped over his chair and fell sprawling on the floor. Fremant picked up the cage and marched right into Safelkty's office, Bellamia following.

Safelkty was remarkably like Essanits in build, a big man, tending toward heaviness. He also had a large, plain face, although alert blue eyes improved matters. A neat beard, showing flecks of white, clung to his jawline. He rose from his seat without haste.

"You were having trouble with my little clerk?" he said, with a slight smile.

"Nothing serious," Fremant replied. He introduced himself and Bellamia. The president was courteous and offered them seats. Fremant then explained the importance of the dog as virtually the last of its species.

Safelkty listened with interest. "Thank you for bringing him this long way. It shows initiative. We'll pop the creature in Cereb. I am told the gadget is now up and running. We can test both the machine and your dog."

"Splendid."

"I can see you have been through much. Be my guests while you are here and stay in our New Hope Hotel."

EIGHT

It was clear that Safelkty set little store by what revelations the dog might provide in the mind-evaluator. Yet he was scientist enough to see they should at least attempt the experiment. For Fremant's part, he rejoiced that here was a man who appeared not to be a bully, and who received them with courtesy. Bellamia and he were installed in a comfortable room in the newly built hotel.

A mixture of relief and weariness overcame them. Both sank together into a deep sleep, in which numerous strange dreams drifted like phantoms from scenes of old plays.

Once more, almost with a sense of faint, faded pleasure at its familiarity, he was back in the grand dilapidated edifice, HARM, containing its whispers and echoes whenever he moved, like the murmurings of the past—a past he never entirely possessed.

And the heavy woman, the officer broad in the beam, was there, explaining again that he was free to go once he signed the release document. She had wheeled in her trolley and checked him medically. She had injected 20 cc of a strange liquid into his veins and had presented him with another copy of the document.

The injection made him at once giddy and exuberant. He signed the document without bothering to read it over again. I, Paul Fadhil Abbas Ali . . .

Pushing the trolley aside, the janitor woman took his arm to propel him forward, as if he had shown some reluctance to leave, perhaps mistaking his feebleness for unwillingness. Or perhaps she thought he was feigning weakness. Certainly it seemed to him that everything was unfolding as dumb show. His walk toward the door of the room was a mere drift.

"So you admit I'm not guilty," he said in a dreamy fashion, mumbling.

"If you were guilty, you'd be leaving as a heap of bones in a black sack."

"Black sack. Black sack, yes."

Then they were in a corridor, still drifting. He could hear neither his own footsteps nor hers. They stopped at a cubbyhole, where his watch and a few trifling belongings were handed over to him. The assistant there smiled at him, even shook his hand as if they were old friends and, smiling, said something Fremant did not hear.

They were at the door, the door to the outside world. A guard hastened with great sloth to fling it open. The door swung back on its hinges without a sound. And there was the street, an ordinary street with pavements on either side of the road and railings on the opposite side. And beyond the railings a neat hedge, showing signs of autumn. Everything was orderly. There were lampposts. Double yellow lines. A car passed, and an old man in a hat was walking along slowly with a white dog on a lead. He knew—he knew with a burst of joy—this was not Syria, not Uzbekistan, but London.

On the top step, the janitor woman turned, put her arms around him, and kissed him on the lips in farewell. He felt her rimless glasses touch his cheek.

"Good luck, dearie!" she said.

She retreated. The great door closed behind her. He was standing alone in the street, aware of the cool air on his face.

He made no move. He could not believe he was free. Although he expected every moment that the door would reopen and they would drag him back into the prison, he made no attempt to leave the spot.

A small car, a shabby Renault Clio, drove up and stopped close by. A young man got out and came briskly to Paul's side. Paul did not recognize him.

"I'm Ned," he said. "Sorry I'm late, the traffic's hell all down Marylebone Road. The government's giving away ice creams to all immigrants. They phoned to say you could be collected at eleven a.m." He glanced at his watch. "Gosh, it's now twenty to twelve—sorry!"

None of this did he understand. He muttered the words "twenty to twelve" over and over, puzzled by them.

His faculties returned when Ned remarked, "Jump in, old chum. Doris is waiting for you."

"She's dead," he heard his own voice saying.

"No, no, Doris is fine. Are you okay?"

But before he could rejoin his wife, the whole scene faded away. He woke in the bed next to Bellamia in the New Hope Hotel, crying with dismay to be back.

...

THEY PRESENTED THEMSELVES, with the dog, before the government offices. After a long delay, Safelkty arrived, apologizing
briefly. At first his manner was lofty and abstracted. He gave
lengthy orders to an attendant, taking no notice of his visitors.

He looked with approval at the caged dog before greeting
them in an amiable way.

His carriage came immediately, a smart vehicle, its panels
gleaming, pulled by two of the humped insect-horses, gaudily
dressed with plumes.

"We are working on horseless carriages," Safelkty remarked
as they all climbed in and were seated. "Motors are being designed. You'll notice my carriage has the new rubber wheels?"

"Are you comfortable?" he asked Bellamia. His manner was
one of warm friendliness, which immediately won Fremant and
Bellamia over. "How did you find the hotel?"

Safelkty was one who behaved with good form when he remembered to do so. He looked upon himself as a good statesman
and a good man. Whether his decisions were, in themselves,
moral or immoral, whether good or ill would result from them,
was a matter of indifference to him. It was for this reason that people regarded him, rightly, as decisive.

He pointed out developments and improvements in Stygia
City as they bowled along.

"It is our Renaissance," he said proudly.

Fremant did not know the word but recognized its intent and
felt delighted to know so great a man.

"You see how clean everywhere is?"

Fremant had not noticed.

"Haven is a filthy hole." Safelkty waved out of the window at a bystander as he spoke.

"Not really . . ."

"I have my reports." He stuck his thumbs into the top of his jeans. "It's a filthy hole thanks to religion. The religious believe they will die and go to a cleaner world, so they don't mind filth in this one."

"I wasn't aware that was the case."

"It *is* the case. I'm *telling* you. Some fools think that when you die you go to a place called Heaven, full of hymns and clouds—or that you get fifty virgins all to yourself. Well, let me tell you, that's all a load of garbage. When you die, your body starts stinking and decaying into a vile mess, okay? It's a scientific *fact*."

"Mmmm."

"I'm telling you, your body decays into a vile mess. No Heaven, no Paradise. See? Do I make myself clear?"

"But it's claimed that the spirit—"

Safelkty's jaw set. "I don't need any argument. I'm *telling* you." Bellamia nudged Fremant to keep quiet.

They reached the great bulk of the *New Worlds* within minutes. It towered over a new addition, a domed building attached to the ship. "We have new workshops here," Safelkty explained as they entered the smoky confines.

Men were at work constructing engines and engine parts. A great roaring came from their benches. Safelkty explained briefly that they worked on what he called "treejuice." He said that Stygia had once, in the days before the Disaster, millions of years back, been heavily forested. With the pressure of the soil and rock on them, those dead forests had been turned into a combustible liquid; this treejuice was now being harnessed to work for them.

They passed into the interior of the ship itself. As they took an elevator, Safelkty again had a word of explanation, saying that his scientists believed the ship had functioned by something he called "gravedy."

Finally they came to a chamber where several men and women were working. However absorbed they were in their work, all snapped to attention when Safelkty entered. Jovially he insisted they continue with their valuable work. He then summoned an old man, by name Tolsteem, to explain their objectives to his visitors.

"Well, this is Operation Cereb, so called," Tolsteem began nervously. "Under our leader, Lord Safelkty, we have forged ahead. We now have good motive power, which before we lacked. And, by the way, I think we did meet once before."

He glanced anxiously at the leader before continuing. "The question of consciousness was a mystery throughout the ages on Earth, finally solved only recently. We now know that consciousness is at least in part a chemical reaction—or interaction, I should say—which occurs in the cerebral cortex, where are sited those chemicals which drive its functioning. Even small creatures, even insects, lacking a cerebral cortex, nevertheless have a certain similar neural resource and marginal awareness—"

"Keep it short, Tolsteem," said Safelkty. "I do not have all day."

Tolsteem began to wring his hands nervously as he continued.

"To cut an interesting story too short, then, we have developed the original mind-evaluator, and can now focus on any conscious activity in any mind by replication of the chemical responses, agitated by a small electrical current, such that the process can be reproduced, externally, on a screen—"

"As we are about to demonstrate," said Safelkty, snapping his fingers with impatience. Other assistants had removed the captive dog from its cage and strapped it into the Cereb apparatus. The dog, in its anxiety, was projecting faint little mothlike signals which seemed to smolder, then writhe into nonexistence almost as soon as they emerged.

"It can't speak, having no vocal cords," said Safelkty. "Instead, it gives forth these imagoes. I do not believe it will have anything useful to convey to us regarding the Dogover culture."

Once switched on, the machine produced a steady hum. Various overhead lights were turned off, but the screen remained blank. An operator worked a variety of knobs, watching dials, listening carefully to slight alterations in tone.

The screen finally lit. A scatter of symbols crossed it, resembling falling leaves. Next moment a coherent picture emerged.

The audience was looking at something resembling a dance. Naked humans, male and female, were prancing about in a glade. Their movements were clumsy. They appeared joyless. Seated in a crescent on chairs were five of the doglike beings, watching the performance. After a while, their tail-appendages moved, the little fingers of which twiddled together—probably a form of applause, as the dancers then stopped and bowed to their audience.

Confused images followed. Then another picture came clear. Small humans were at work, building a kind of hut, triangular in shape, of a type Fremant recognized. They built rapidly, as if trained, while other humans brought sticks and straw for the building. Two dog-beings looked on from a bank nearby. When the hut was thatched and finished, the humans adorned it with flowers, yellow and blue. They stood back and fell silent. A large dog-being, its body decorated with similar yellow and blue flowers, approached. It nodded to the right and to the left, sending out a string of elaborate signals, while the humans bowed. It entered the hut.

"Stop!" ordered Safelkty, in a loud voice. "Stop this nonsense. It's a fake!"

Tolsteem, who had appeared so nervous and submissive only moments earlier, now spoke up sharply.

"Of course it's not a fake! Allow us to continue, Master. This is most interesting."

"I order you to switch off the Cereb!"

Tolsteem stood up to confront his leader. "No, sir, you must see this. You are a scientist. You must respect the truth!"

"I do not respect this rubbish!"

"This 'rubbish,' sir—as you call it—clearly indicates that Stygia once had a culture where the pygmies were inferior to the species we have mistakenly called 'dogs.' We have to face up to the fact."

"You're being confused by one wretched dog's imagining."

"No, sir. We are viewing a record from its memory of times that were. You forget that we seem to have been cast upon a planet where the insects have dominance and have adopted many intelligent and semi-intelligent forms.

"The human-like forms here had no such good fortune. The 'insects,' as we must call them, may well have had many million years' head start on them. Why should we have assumed that the great impulse toward life would always take the same pathways across the universe? Watch on, I say! Truth is a bitter herb, a cure for illusion—and pride!"

Safelkty seemed almost to burst with suppressed anger but

said nothing in response. He gestured abruptly as a sign that the evaluator should continue.

Other scenes played. Each indicated that Tolsteem's analysis was correct. The dog-beings kept the small humans as slaves and playthings. In one scene, a group of six humanoids were judged by their masters to have committed a crime. They stood in a circle, linking arms around shoulders, looking inward and down. And then they died, killing themselves by voluntary stoppage of their hearts. The viewers watched this strange act in silence, disconcerted.

Happier scenes followed. Newborn dogs, their tails waving freely, played among the humans. Humans cuddled and ran about with the baby dogs in their arms. Again, dogs and humans splashed about freely in a river. So secure was the dog-species in its supremacy that the supremacy was not insisted upon. Such episodes of frolic touched the watchers greatly.

In yet another scene, again there was a celebration of some kind. Dogs joined with the humans, frisking with them, enveloping the scene with ribbons of bright symbols in many fascinating shapes—"Oh, it must be their sort of music!" Bellamia exclaimed—when some giants appeared. The giants were not clearly seen, so that their forms were distorted; but all who watched realized who these monsters were. The monsters advanced in a furious wave, killing every living being indiscriminately. Only a few of the dogs, running for safety, managed to escape the slaughter.

"How cruel!" Fremant exclaimed.

"Yes, we have much to answer for," said Tolsteem, and he switched off the machine.

Safelkty turned on his heels and left.

OLD TOLSTEEM AND HIS COLLEAGUES began an eager discussion of what they had seen. "One can completely understand how an insect might evolve over generations into full consciousness. The fact that it somewhat resembles a terrestrial dog is neither here nor there. The brain waves we have registered are uncommonly like those we see in the human brain," said one old fellow.

"Having no lungs per se, these giant insects couldn't speak," another said in response. "So they developed a mode of visual signal response."

"Yes, very elegant in many aspects," another agreed.

"A necessary response to the environment," said the youth who had operated the machine. "Their mix of superimposed frequences seldom varies from between about twenty to forty hertz."

"Can we say, then, that the dog-beings acquired full consciousness?" asked Tolsteem. "That would imply that various regions of their brains interconnect, always alert for the—the, er, continuous conference command we call consciousness. Even terrestrial insects had the rudiments of such systems, we understand.

"All told, this entails a staggering overturning of our previous ignorant convictions." He chuckled. "One quite sees why our beloved leader marched out in a huff . . .

"It will be interesting to dissect this creature's brain."

He gestured to the dog still strapped into the machine, and now looking bedraggled.

Fremant called out in alarm. "You must let him go, return

him to the wild! You have just proved that he is our equal in intellect—and he's the last of his race. You must let him go free!"

"Oh, we can't do that," said Tolsteem, with a demure smile. "He's much too precious to us. We are scientific people, my friend."

WHEN FREMANT AND BELLAMIA LEFT, to return to their hotel room, Bellamia clutched his arm.

"Don't fret. It had to happen. Had to. We killed 'em all off. What does one more matter? Don't be upset. Let's get something to eat."

"You realize, don't you, that a whole little universe has been destroyed through man's cruelty?"

She made *tut-tut*ting noises. "Men are like that, my dear. It's useless to fret. Useless. I'll find you something nice to eat."

Fremant emitted a wild laugh. "Jupers!—And women are like *that*!" But he went along with her.

He recognized the good sense in what she said. Yet it did not touch him.

He had to accept his limited capacities. Those stronger than he had controlled him. He knew from personal experience the mental powers of the dog-people; why had he allowed this individual to be caged? Why had he brought it unquestioningly to Stygia City, only to let it be experimented on? He hated himself for doing it.

He thought he had only been doing "the right thing." Instead he had denied what was good and true in his nature. It was this understanding that kept him awake in his bed that night.

Toss and turn as he might, he could not escape the pain of a profound truth: that under the stresses of normal life, he who had once been—or had regarded himself as—an upright and honest young fellow, had allowed falsehood in. Falsehood had taken over, as dry rot takes over an old house, to its ultimate decay.

Despite himself, he began thinking of Doris, the sweetly trusting woman he had married. With what disdain he had treated her; and all the while that disdain had been a projection of his own disdain for himself. He had been so eager to demonstrate to the Western world that he was not a . . . not a Muslim. So he had betrayed himself, adopting Western manners, marrying a Western wife, even writing a Western-style novel.

He sat up in startlement in the dark, seeing light. Those throwaway lines in his novel, about the British prime minister being assassinated—his torturers were right, in essence. They reflected his true secret hatred for what he had become, for suppressing his true nature under the pressure of "doing the right thing."

Fatigue freed him at last from his thoughts.

NINE

SOMEONE WAS SHAKING HIS SHOULDER and saying, gently, "Wake up."

"I wasn't asleep," he said.

"You're free to go now. Your name has been cleared."

Yet nothing was clear. He moved in a mist. His jailers seemed cordial. One helped him on with his jacket. The woman he had encountered before put the document of clearance in front of him. He signed without thinking.

"There's a good boy," she said, making off with the document with her broad-beamed, complacent walk.

He had made no reference to the death of his wife. He was led along a familiar corridor. There a man in an apron was pasting posters to the corridor wall. One poster said WAKE UP! GOD DOES NOT EXIST. The poster currently being stuck up read ONLY FOOLS AND TURDS BELIEVE THAT ALLAH WAS NOT A FOOL AND A TURD.

At a small kiosk at the end of the corridor his trifling possessions were restored to him, including his biometric ID card.

"Good luck, sir!" said the man behind the counter. "Have a nice day."

Another guard led him through coded doors to a guarded outer door. As a man was unlocking it, Paul asked him, "What country are we in?"

"You'll find out soon enough," said the guard with a chuckle. He opened the door a foot or two and pushed the released prisoner out of prison. The door slammed behind him.

The rush of a small breeze, the blood in his head, the unsteadiness of his legs, the terror of something unstated . . .

He was dazed by daylight, overcome by the freshness of the air, the pure feel of it in his lungs. He sat down abruptly on the step.

On his side of the road stood imposing terraced houses. On the opposite side of the road were iron railings, painted black. Beyond them was what looked like a park, with people playing a friendly game of cricket. He could hear the familiar sound of bat against ball.

There was a side street with a road sign, white on black, announcing that this was Canterbury Walk. He knew beyond doubt he was in London.

The relief was considerable. "London," he whispered to himself. It was a city he had once loved, where he imagined he felt at home . . .

He looked up at the building in which he had been imprisoned. Its impressively ornate façade had been wounded by neglect. Part of a stone balcony had fallen away. Other stone had crumbled. Windows, the eyes of the building, had been boarded up.

A modest brass plate attached to one of the pillars by the side of the prison doors caught his eye. He shuffled over to look at it. The plate read, in elegant lettering, HOSTILE ACTIVITIES RE-SEARCH MINISTRY.

Again he sank down on the steps, trying to reflect on how disastrously the state of the world had declined in so few years, but coherent thought was beyond him.

Although he could hear police sirens distantly, the road was quiet. Few cars passed. He was content to slump there on the step, unable to consider his next move, just breathing the fresh air.

A car arrived from the left and drew up at the curb. A young man of about Paul's age and of good appearance jumped out and ran to him.

"Sorry I'm so delayed, Ali!" he said as he clutched Paul's hand. "Salaam Aleikum! The street is blocked at the far end by the cops. There have been more explosions from the extremists. Some women killed, I heard. How are you, are you okay? Can you walk?"

Ali — Paul! — was deeply confused. Had he not left the prison previously? — When, unlikely as it might seem, the janitor woman with the rimless glasses had kissed him good-bye? Had he not been previously met?

And now, again — were his personae breaking down, and with them his whole complex personality?

"Where's Bellamia?" he managed to ask.

"You're free of that place now. Got to get you home fast. The city's in chaos."

Paul allowed himself to be helped to his feet. He recognized the man as a friend but could not recall his name.

"How long have I been away?" he asked faintly, but the friend was talking, going on about how difficult the bombings had made life for the Muslim community. He could not tell which he hated most, the British or the extremists. As he laughed unhappily, spit flew from his mouth.

"Let's get away from here," he said, bundling Paul into the back of his car, which Paul recognized as an ancient Volvo wagon, although he still could not recall the name of his rescuer.

"Where are we going?" he asked.

The rescuer did not answer, too involved in executing a U-turn and then accelerating in the direction from which he had come. They drove within sight of Paddington Station, where the building had suffered a major explosion. A fire was blazing furiously, despite the attentions of firefighters. Fire engines, police cars, and ambulances crowded the roads nearby. Helicopters roared overhead.

A mob of people, roped off, stood on the nearby pavement. Almost silent, they stared at the conflagration. Paramedics were carrying bodies away. The nearby Bishop's Bridge Road was closed.

The Volvo was stopped. The police were courteous enough, but grim, no-nonsense. They scrutinized ID cards and questioned both men, making them get out of the car to be searched. They were allowed to go on their way.

"Sorry to hold you up, sir," one said politely.

"Bloody liar," the driver said under his breath as he put his foot down.

They drove through the mazes of West Kilburn to Kensal Town. Paul became dizzied by the speed of the car and the changes of direction. He closed his eyes and allowed his mind to wander. His head ached overpoweringly.

When he opened his eyes, they had stopped on Southern

Drive, outside a pleasant-looking suburban house with a glossy-leafed laurel in its tiny strip of front garden. His friend helped him from the car.

"Where are we?"

"You're home, you idiot! Doris is waiting for you."

"Doris?"

As is frequently the case with those who attend the sick, the friend did not bother to answer but hurried him to the front door. Resting Paul against the low porch railing, he rang the bell. A head protruded from an upper window.

"Oh, Palab, it's you, safe back!"—spoken with relief. "I'll come down."

In a minute, the sound of bolts being withdrawn and the door opening. There stood Doris—a somewhat altered Doris, fatter and with strands of silver in her hair, but still Doris. A Doris with dark patches under her eyes.

"Paul, my darlin'! It's you! Heaven be praised!" Doris had converted to the Islamic faith to please her husband, but she retained some of her Irish turns of phrase.

Paul fell into her arms, hugging and kissing her in feeble fashion.

"Holy Mother—how you stink, love!" she exclaimed. "Come along in. What on earth have they been doing to you?"

So the sadists in the prison had lied to him, saying she was dead, just in order to make his existence that much more miserable . . .

"Allah knows what we've been through. It's a terrible time to be alive and kicking. If you knew what they put me through, Paul dear . . . It was humiliating. I've not recovered. I'm as nervous as a raspberry jelly and all. I doubt I'll ever recover. Come in and sit your poor self down, and I'll get you a nice cup of tea. Do you want to have a lie-down?"

He was taken into the overfurnished back room. From the window he saw the roof of a train trundling slowly by on the main line.

The friend addressed as Palab agreed with Doris. "It was shameful. We're all afraid of arrest. The cops are so damned racist—they long to get hold of you." Turning to Paul, he contin-ued: "And I'm sure you remember that nice harmless Socrani family who used to live down the road? The government has now forcibly deported them to Iraq, just because he got in with a forged passport."

"Socrani was a Kurd," Doris reminded him.

"It's true, he was a bloody Kurd. Still, I liked him."

"How long have I been away, Doris?" Paul asked faintly.

"I tell you, Ali," said Palab, overriding the question, "things are bad for all of us. You need a doctor, I can see that. We all need psychotherapists . . ."

"You need a bath, that's what," said Doris, hands on hips. "I've had a lot of treatment. Not that it's done me much good. And I keep on putting on the weight. It's all these comfort foods, as they call them, but I can't knock it off. Cherry cake, Madeira cake dunked in cream—you name it. It seems I need it. Better that than the booze . . . I'm off the booze now, love. Still and all, thanks to Allah you're back safe and sound! Just rest yourself for a moment and I'll bring you a nice cup of tea and a jammy dodger. You like jammy dodgers, don't you?"

"We buy the packets cheap from Mrs. Singh," Palab ex-plained. "Her husband drives a bus and it seems he can get them cheap from the back of the supermarket. We don't do badly as far as food's concerned, I'll say that. Everyone round here helps each other. There's a pair of cops patrol here regularly now. You'll see them. They're not bad blokes as these things go. One of them's a black man, name of Kelvin. He's pretty sympathetic."

"Could I have a drink of water, do you think?" Paul asked. "It's the shock of everything, of being free, of finding you alive and well, Doris . . ."

"Alive, but not well," she said firmly. "Settle down there on that sofa and sleep it off. I'll bring you another cushion."

He sighed. He could not believe he was free. He closed his eyes.

THE WATER WAS RUNNING OVER HIS FACE. He let it run. He would willingly drown as long as that cool water kept on running. It ran from his forehead down over both of his closed eyes, alongside his nose, over his lips, and down the line of his jaw into his shirt.

"You're awake, sweetie. I know it. Open eyes . . ." Not Doris's voice. A huskier voice, equally beloved. "Bellamia!" he exclaimed. As he opened his eyes, she ceased pouring water and kissed him on his wet lips.

"You had a shock, sweetie! Get up and walk around." She put a hand under his arm and helped him up.

Fremant laughed shakily. "Certainly did have a shock. We all had a shock. You realize we humans have destroyed a whole culture. The battle of the cultures . . . Is that nothing?"

Bellamia sighed deeply. "Jupers, why do I ever love you? Battle of the cultures, indeed! Cheer up, will you?"

"Islamic and Christian."

"You're talking rubbish."

"Oh, Bellamia, how I love your blind good sense!"

"Blind good nothing, man!" But suddenly somehow she was not there with him. Her voice came from far away, and there were other voices.

He held her at arm's length, regarding her, smiling.

"Listen," she said, "you want to do something, Free? Go and speak to crowds in the square. Speak in the square! You can tell people about this big big guilt, eh?"

He thought he just might do as she suggested.

Another Dimoff was coming. The two of them huddled in their small room together, sleeping much of the time. In his waking periods, Fremant devised a placard and reflected on what he would say when he addressed the crowds.

When daylight returned, he set off for the main square. Bellamia came with him. This time, it was her turn to express doubt and confusion.

"I ought not have made you do this. We'll get ourselves killed."

They went to what was called, under the new dispensation, Square One, a place through which many pedestrians passed, going to work at this early hour.

On his placard was written HUMAN RASE—GILTY?

Fremant called to all the passersby, asking them if they were aware of the crime that had been committed in their name— that is, the genocide of the Dogovers.

A thin, haggard woman clutching a small child of indeterminate sex stopped to listen a moment.

"Awright," she said, "maybe we did kill 'em all off, but we had to. Anyway, it's all over now, so what's the use of making a fuss about it? Best to forget all about it."

Another woman, following, shouted, "Get outta here! We don't wanna hear it!"

A young burly man with bare, muscular arms, said, "You stupid bastard, it was kill or be killed."

Many people had similar remarks to make.

Only one man, lame and walking with a stick, said, "You're right, my friend. Us humans, we're a rotten lot. But why put yourself in danger by saying so?"

Bellamia clung to Fremant's arm. "He's right, sweet. There's nothing to be gained by trying to preach here. My mistake. Let's go!"

But at that moment, Tolsteem, led by a small boy, came into view. He stopped and surveyed the placard.

"That's not the way to spell *guilty*, young man."

"No one else has complained."

"That does not prove your spelling to be correct. You may be the only one to think we Stygians are guilty of genocide. I myself don't, though that's not to say you are incorrect in making your protest."

"So you will support me?" asked Fremant eagerly.

Tolsteem shook his head, making his shaggy locks tremble. "You think the grass is green? The color is just a quantum side effect. Subtle interactions between atoms of chlorophyll in the grass create light of a certain wavelength. Our clever little brains transform this wavelength into 'greenness.' "

"What's that got to do with anything?"

"Everything! What you think you perceive as guilt, the rest of us see as survival."

"But we *are* guilty."

"Forget it, my boy! We have to. It's only the strongest who survive. That's the way the system of existence works."

The boy by his side showed signs of restlessness. "Can't we go home, Grampa?"

As they stood there arguing, four strong young men—among them Tunderkin, who had been a guard in Astaroth's day, immediately recognizable by the scar on his left cheek—came marching rapidly along, armed with staves. Each of the men wore a badge on his dark tunic.

"You're not allowed here!" one shouted as he approached.

"You're causing a disturbance," shouted his twin.

"I bid you good day," said Tolsteem, hastily quitting the scene, the small boy trotting at his side, looking back anxiously.

"I am allowed to be here!" said Fremant. "It's a serious question I'm asking."

"It's a lot of bluggeration," the man responded, wielding his stick. "And you better blugger off!"

"Get out, you ruffian! I've every right—"

The stave, swung with accuracy and strength, caught him on his neck, just below the skull, precisely where, in another world, he had been hit before.

He seemed to hear bells ringing as he fell, and to see a stream of sparks, emanating from nowhere, pursuing him into the darkness.

THE HOUSE ON SOUTHERN DRIVE was well-occupied. Doris Fadhill supplemented her meager income as a part-time worker at a local Youth Reclamation Center by renting out her frontupstairs room.

When Paul roused, he sat up, not moving for a while, feeling glad to be there. He went to hang up his jacket on a hook screwed to a wooden strip, but the wood had crumbled away at one end.

"Don't bother," Palab said. "It's the bloody woodworm. Give us your jacket." He tossed it over the back of a chair. Doris came rushing from the rear of the house and flung her bare arms round Paul's neck, crying and kissing him. They embraced almost like wrestlers, only slowly becoming more coherent, smiling into each other's faces.

She took him into the kitchen and poured him a glass of Special Brew.

"Tea?" he asked. He needed Bellamia.

She looked at him in puzzlement. "You're not well. I must get you to bed and look after you."

As Doris explained, the other occupants of the house were Palab and his aged mother, old Fatima. Fatima and Palab had fled from Iraq many years ago. Fatima remained veiled from head to foot and spoke no English.

Once a week, with the aid of her stick, she would get herself to the mosque in Kensal Town. Sometimes Doris escorted the poor old thing to the doors of the mosque. No one harmed her.

Fatima met an old friend at the mosque. The two of them would sit most of the day in a nearby café over two small cups of coffee. The friend smoked heavily, and would occasionally give Fatima one of her cigarettes. She claimed that these cigarettes were specially imported from Iran.

This friend talked about her daughter, who wore short skirts and had given up the veil. She was doing well in local radio. Or they would speak about life in the village they had once known, where it was hot and it rarely rained—not like this horrible country they were in—and they kept a few chickens. The friend had been very ill as a child. As a result she had had a hard labor in delivering her one daughter, and her insides had come out with the baby. And to think that that same girl had now given up the veil and wore short skirts almost showing her *puccta*. Things had come to a pretty pass indeed . . . On that, both agreed.

Apart from this weekly excursion, Fatima scarcely stirred from her room on Southern Drive, except to come and sit downstairs in the evening and share in the evening meal. She ate sparingly, not liking the "English food," such as spaghetti or chicken tikka, which the others enjoyed.

"She's a bit of a nuisance," said Doris cheerfully, "but she helps pay the rates."

The evening meal was finished and Paul and his wife were washing up in the little back kitchen. Palab was out, visiting friends.

Fatima sat by the window in the front room, staring vacantly into the street. With one claw, she clutched the velour curtain, shaking it in tune to the disease that was slowly destroying her. The TV talked to itself, unheeded, behind her.

As he dried the dishes, Paul tried to recount what had been said during his visit to the local hospital, where he had had an appointment to see a Dr. Roger Thomas. "He has no surname," Paul explained. "He was most kind and considerate and wise. A good listener. I have often told you about how my father would beat me. One day he threw me out of the window into the courtyard."

"Oh, that horrible man!" Doris exclaimed.

Paul fell silent, chewing over his bitterness.

Then he said, "He was in authority over me. All men in authority, however they begin, become hateful with time."

He had liked what he said when he said it, but Doris ignored the remark.

"Were you badly hurt when he slung you out like that?"

"I was unconscious for two days. I hurt my head. When I awoke, I thought I was in another place. I went to live with my aunt for a week. These things, Dr. Roger explained, contributed to my dissociative identity disorder. He showed me diagrams and—what's it called?—scans. But it does not explain how I have lived on the distant planet of Stygia, which is at least as real as—"

He broke off, interrupting himself. And was silent, thinking. He recalled Dr. Roger saying, with a certain pleasure in his dry old voice, that there was no explanation for the riddle of human consciousness. As far as he knew, it was an accident.

Putting down the plate he was drying, he told Doris, "Yes, Dr. Roger gave me the example of a goldfish in a bowl. The goldfish has no chance of understanding the world beyond his bowl. Since we are all contained within the bowl of our limited joint consciousness, it follows—"

He was interrupted by a cry of terror from the old woman in the front room.

Paul ran to see what was the matter, dishcloth in hand. The TV still blazed. He glimpsed, in passing, a shot of a broken building, surrounded by mobs of men in uniform.

A yellow subtitle read, LONDON: BREAKING NEWS.

Fatima, gibbering, pointed across the narrow strip of front garden to the pavement, where four men were advancing on the

house. Wearing bulky heavy-duty uniforms. All four were holding weapons at the ready.

"Jupers! They're after me again!" Paul exclaimed. He began
to run from the room. "This time they'll kill me, for sure!"

Doris grabbed his arm.

"They can't be after you, Paul! You've not been out of their
clutches a week. Speak to them, reassure the bloody sods!"

"Speak? You're daft . . ." He broke loose from her grip and
ran to the back door. He pulled it open. Men stood in the dark
garden, weapons raised. One shone a bright beam of light at
him. He slammed the door, dazzled and in terror.

Hammering started at the front door. He ran frantically up
the stairs.

Doris, terrified, unlocked the front door and stared out.

One of the four men had positioned himself to watch the
window. The other three men crowded into the porch.

"Out of the way, lass. We are here to arrest a man known as
Paul or Ali Fadhil."

"What do you want with him?"

"Questioning. Move out the way."

"Paul's not in."

The speaker pushed her aside and entered the house with a
second man. The third stood guard in the porch.

"What's he done? *What's he done?*" Doris shrieked. Fatima
was screaming in the front room. The men rushed in upon her.

"Who's this old witch?" the leader asked Doris.

"She's only a lodger. She doesn't speak English. She won't
understand anything you say."

"Another fucking Muslim . . ."

The remark didn't stop the leader from trying to question Fatima. He took her wrist and shook it. She screamed and hit him with her free hand.

He turned away indifferently, letting Fatima fall to her knees on the floor. The two men then searched the downstairs rooms, calling loudly for Paul to give himself up.

They ran upstairs. They cornered Paul on the upstairs landing. He stood rigid by the banister rail, raising his hands in the traditional pose of surrender. The leader advanced on him while the second man covered his partner.

Pale about the lips, Paul said, indistinctly, "Do not harm me. I have been harmed enough. I did you no harm."

"Come quietly, then!"

Paul kicked out and caught the oncoming man on the knee. As the man bent over involuntarily, Paul struck him in the face and forced him against the banister. The frail, worn structure broke. The man dropped his gun and grasped at a piece of railing. It broke in his clutches. He was already beginning to fall. As he dropped, his fellow officer opened fire on Paul.

The house filled with noise, yells, shouts, the dull sound of a body striking the tiled corridor in the hall. Then silence.

"Paul! Are you okay?" cried Doris in a weak voice. She held on to a doorjamb to steady her trembling. The man in the porch entered the house. Once inside, he stood menacingly, looking grim, saying nothing, ready to shoot if need be.

The man on the upper landing peered over and shouted down to his mate, "Have a look at Stan. See if he's okay."

He then knelt and put handcuffs on Paul. Paul lay there, writhing, teeth gritted against pain. A bullet had shattered the femur of his right leg.

"Get up," he was told.

Paul struggled to obey. A splinter of bone had spiked through the flesh of his thigh, tearing the fabric of his jeans.

The soldier down below was calling for an ambulance on his mobile. "Stop that fucking woman screaming," he told Doris. She vanished into the front room.

Paul was dragged to his feet. His captor, keeping a firm hold of him, forced him to hop downstairs. He left a thin trail of blood as he went.

"What have I done?" he gasped. "Where are you taking me?"

His captor, shaking him violently, turned a red, enraged face to him.

"The prime minister has jus' been sodding well assassinated — just like you planned."

"What? I've done nothing . . ."

"A mortar shell was fired through an upper window of Number Ten, you bastard. The PM was killed instantly — just like you fucking planned . . ."

"Oh, Allah the Merciful . . ."

He glimpsed Doris's frightened face, chalk white, as they dragged him out into the London darkness where so much had gone wrong and so many wrongs were done . . .

EVEN AS HE WAS BEING BEATEN UP in the police van, he could hear a faint voice speaking in a monotone. He could not recall the name of the speaker. The man was arguing for the necessity of power to control populations. The leader had to be strong; he must not be misled by mistaken principles of mercy; mercy was often a disguise for weakness. The opinions of populations needed to be directed toward a positive end. That made sense.

He had now won the position of head of state and would not tolerate any negative talk of genocide.

Threats to stability had to be stamped out, wherever they occurred. One had to put a stop to such dangerous thoughts. Nevertheless, he, the mighty Safelkty, had been advised by Tolsteem that you were a thinking man and that among a nation of the ignorant an intellect such as yours was necessary.

You were required to make certain revisions in your attitude toward life, and would be trained; after which, you would be elected to a position of authority.

We were traveling, four of us, through beautiful unspoiled countryside. We admitted to a guilty pleasure because this halcyon
wilderness made us think of what England must once have
looked like, in the Middle Ages, before clocks chimed or modernity was heard of.

Our vehicle climbed a low hill. As we came down into the
vale on the other side, we saw a gaggle of people, mainly
women, standing under a magnificent tree. A black horse was
hanging by its neck from a branch. Blowflies buzzed everywhere. A man with a large knife was cutting strips of flesh from
the horse's body and selling them to the women. This was in
Albania, shortly after the dictator Enver Hoxha had died.

Maturity: Perhaps maturity means finding a way to move
with equanimity between the contrapuntal intricacies of joy and
anguish, action and thought, fire and calm, love and dismay—
all those things that underlie our engagement with experience.
Not to be indifferent. Not to be indifferent to the sight we witnessed in Albania: to feel for the poverty to which those women
had been reduced, to feel for the savagery of the butcher, perhaps to feel for the remorseless unwinding of history.

Boyhood: Enlivened and enlightened by reading editor John
Campbell's *Astounding*. I read much else besides, but it was on
Astounding that my imagination mainly fed. My style came

from elsewhere: from Hardy, from Swift, from Dickens, and from the poems of Alexander Pope.

I was always glad of the umbrella that the science fiction field provided. Most of my friends hail from there. Only gradually have I come to believe that many writers were reduced to hacking strips off an old carcass.

My claim, my passport, is that I am a Steppenwolf. But then, all true writers are Steppenwolves. They live amid human societies—and some societies are decidedly more desirable than others—but always they have their quarrels, their differences. *HARM*'s another such a one.

A CONVERSATION WITH BRIAN W. ALDISS

Del Rey: Science fiction has a tradition of dystopian novels that comment on current political events, Orwell's *1984* and Bradbury's *Fahrenheit 451* being two of the most famous. Do you see *HARM* as being in that tradition?

Brian W. Aldiss: It never occurred to me. *HARM* is the sort of book I have been writing over the last half-century. *Non-Stop, Greybeard, Forgotten Life, Super-State* . . . all protest against something, generally against the shortcomings of human life itself. Of course I have read [Sir Thomas] More, *Brave New World*, and all the rest of the famous utopias.

DR: Why choose science fiction as the genre in which to critique the way that governments have responded to 9/11? Doesn't that risk diluting your message in ways that a realistic novel would not? For example, couldn't critics dismiss your arguments by saying that *HARM* is a fantasy, its main character a man with a personality disorder?

BA: I take your point. I have nothing against the realistic novel, but I am more practiced at SF. If people read *HARM* as SF, they may dismiss it as "mere SF," as they so often do. I don't feel like that about SF—and some of the truths of my story may linger, even with the scoffers. To be made uneasy is the beginning of enlightenment.

DR: Why did you choose to give your character this mental illness—was it simply a technical move, to better facilitate the translation back and forth between the two main realities of the novel: Earth and the insect-dominated world of Stygia?

BA: My character Paul's divided personality suffers another division: he is British, he is a Muslim. What ultimately gets him into trouble is that he "presumes" to write a Wodehousian novel. I believe that in the end he perceives he would have been better to accept the fact that he could be both British and Muslim (a question radiating some unease on both sides just now).

DR: One element of the novel I especially enjoyed was all the nods to the history of SF, from the pure pulp to the literary, that contribute to the reconstituted culture of Stygia. There's the name itself, with its echoes of Robert E. Howard, but also places like Seldonia and characters such as Tolsteem. And of course this breaking down and reconstituting the past of the genre into humorous and often ironic permutations is also present on deeper levels. It's obvious that you got a lot of pleasure out of this aspect of what is otherwise a very dark book.

BA: Stygia as a name comes from Milton's *Paradise Lost* (a poem quoted later). There some can be simultaneously almost-alive and almost-dead—rather similar to Paul's situation. Of course, Paul's character is such that torture—which he perceives to be unjust—facilitates his refuge in another place, if indeed it is a refuge. On Stygia too, as on Earth, there is religious struggle.

As far as I recall, I have never read any Robert Howard—a possible character defect—although of course I have read in his tradition. In that tradition, there are generally monsters to contend with. Contending with insects is even worse, certainly more itchy. Don't forget that literature derives not only from other literature but from life itself. I spent many years in the wilds of the East, wherein itchiness was a prominent feature of existence.

DR: As you point out, there are Miltonian echoes and allusions in the book. Why is Milton an important writer to you, especially in connection with *HARM*?

BA: Every author owes obeisance to some other writer or writers. I have reviewed well over a thousand books. Unfortunately, I arrived too late to review *Paradise Lost* ("Unputdownable," I might have said). But I have read and admired the mighty poem—as did Mary Shelley. Does it lend a certain grandeur to one's imagination? You tell me.

DR: How much is the main character, Paul Fadhil Abbas Ali, an alter-ego for Brian Aldiss? The similarity of names seems deliberate . . .

BA: Goodness, I hope Paul is no sort of alter-ego for me! It is true that when I returned to England after that long adolescent sojourn overseas, I had become a stranger in my own country. But for all that . . . no, no.

DR: How close are the England and America of today to the totalitarian near-future that you depict in *HARM*? And are those two countries marching more or less in lockstep toward that future?

BA: I do not accept that England and America are totalitarian. One addresses the public in the belief that they will consciously heed our dreadful sins and—if possible—cure them. Or get voted out. We cannot, I believe, ever break free of our relationship, the U.S. and the U.K., mainly because of the remarkable language we share. Then there's the other thing about the child being father to the man . . .

You now have the Democrats sitting in the seats of the mighty. Perhaps you can make amends for that terrible mistake of invading Iraq—and we for that more humiliating mistake of blindly following your president, the Burning Bush, into that unfortunate land.

DR: For the edification of Americans like me, why did Tony Blair embrace the mission of George W. Bush with such fervor?

BA: Only reluctantly do I cease to admire Tony Blair. He did much that was good for Britain. He was debonair. He sank millions into the National Health Service. He was as much Middle England as Socialist. Did the adulation of the many go to his head? Most likely that wise saying of Lord Acton applies: "Power corrupts, absolute power corrupts absolutely." Perhaps Blair saw in Bush the absolute power he could not help craving. In any case, he became a poodle. Now his popularity drains fast away. We wait wearily to see what he will get up to vis-à-vis the Democrats.

DR: In *HARM*, the writer Paul Fadhil Abbas Ali is arrested because his novel, *Pied Piper of Hament*, contains a joke about the assassination of a British prime minister. As a British citizen of Muslim heritage, Paul is suspected of connections with Islamic terrorists. I'm wondering if this aspect of your novel, the assassination of a prime minister, has drawn any attention from the British authorities.

BA: Sadly, the national atmosphere has become tainted with suspicion. Paul jokes about assassinating the PM to show how far he is from such actions—fatally, of course. (A new report claims that 1,600 young British Muslims are being radicalized and are under surveillance.)

DR: What is the significance of that title, *Pied Piper of Hament*? Although it is not described in detail, Paul's novel seems somewhat similar to *HARM*, in that it is a fantasy with dual realities: another level of recursiveness in your book.

BA: Agreed about recessive realities. There is no particular significance in the title beyond the Browning reference and the fact that rats follow the piper.

DR: Paul is swept up on the flimsiest of pretexts, then subjected to torture that is made even more abhorrent by the vile racism of his interlocutors. Yet isn't there a real danger to the West from Islamic terrorists? Where should the line be drawn in responding to this threat?

BA: Paul arrested on the flimsiest of pretexts? But paranoia is the last refuge of a scoundrel; they may have had Paul under surveillance for some while. The novel opens with our knowing nothing about Paul. As I write, in the U.K. it's the day of the lord mayor's show, with many acts and groups on show (including the formidable Knights of Kazakhstan!) parading through a sunny London, and the sidewalks are crammed with thousands of people. How tempting a target for some mad terrorist with a few pounds of explosives strapped round his chest . . .

Where indeed should a line be drawn?

DR: Were the brutal interrogation scenes of Paul difficult to write?

BA: I enjoyed writing the torture scenes. Possibly prophylactic! I have studied various torture procedures. It has been a European tradition ever since the rack was introduced.

DR: The science fiction elements of *HARM* are startling and brilliant, beginning with the notion that the colonists of Stygia have been transported to that planet with their brain functions and DNA stored in LPRs, or Life Process Reservoirs, and then reconstituted upon arrival in new amalgamations of their previous physical and mental identities. It's as if they've been disassembled, the pieces put into boxes that are shaken up thoroughly, and then put back together willy-nilly. How did you come up with this outrageous idea?

BA: Cogitating on the question of transportation over many lightyears, I came on what seemed to me almost the only solution: to store the individual lives in LPRs. When you think around such ideas, they take on a fake reality; I thought this was the best strategy. Of course it served to break up families and other relationships. The new Stygians are virtually computer compositions (Bellamia expresses some anxieties on this very point). In particular, humans may survive, but the old constitutions and relationships, such as families—the elements that hold our fragile world-ethic together—are destroyed by this long storage.

DR: Perhaps unsurprisingly, given this treatment, most of the reconstituted colonists have suffered degrees of brain damage, making their speech word salads of malapropisms and unconsciously ironic puns. The sheer linguistic dexterity of this reminded me of the delirious Joycean wordplay that characterized your novel *Barefoot in the Head*.

BA: All survivors from the ship are damaged in some way. Wisely, perhaps, I was advised to cut down on the disintegration of language.

DR: Three of your works have been adapted for film: the short story "Supertoys Last All Summer Long" as Spielberg's *Artificial Intelligence*; the novel *Frankenstein Unbound* as Roger Corman's movie of the same name; and *Brothers of the Head*, also given eponymous movie treatment. Have you been pleased with these adaptations? Which is your favorite? And are there any more films in the works?

BA: When you sell a written something-or-other to Hollywood, you should accept that a translation must be made. You have no power over this transformation. Hence the old saying, "Take the money and run." I didn't run. My family and I went to stay in Bellagio on the shores of Lake Como in Italy, to watch the filming. Roger Corman was a genial and generous host. Most of the film, shot in a local palazzo, looks beautiful. There is much to be said for *Frankenstein Unbound*.

I worked with Stanley Kubrick on *Supertoys*, but wanted us to create a new modern myth. Kubrick was set on *Pinocchio*, whereas I could not accept the Blue Fairy (the mere name gave me the whim-whams) or the notion of David somehow becoming a real boy. In the end, Stanley had to kick me out. I don't regret that semi-collaboration; it is a privilege to work with a genius, even a genius in decay. But much of the screenplay of what became *Artificial Intelligence* is illogical and vulgar.

For sheer noise, *Brothers of the Head* beats them all, but holds many fascinations. This company, Marlin Films, with its remarkable screenwriter, Tony Grisoni, have made mockumentaries before. The book of *Brothers* is written in mockumentary style, and thus was comparatively easy to transform to film in like fashion. Not believing in God—a weird idea—I always worry about his imitation, an omniscient narrator in books, so that *Brothers* is written, like the later *White Mars*, by various witnesses. And where did that strategy originate? You can find it in Robert Louis Stevenson's *Strange Case of Dr. Jekyll and Mr. Hyde*.

DR: *HARM* is also concerned with the link between religious belief, oppression, and violence. Recently Richard Dawkins has written a critique of religious belief, expressing the opinion that, in the post–9/11 world, the dangers of this belief (or, if you prefer, faith) far outweigh any benefits. Nor is he referring simply to Islam. Can you address this aspect of *HARM*?

BA: Oxford is a city attracting many intelligent people. We have multiculturalism here without too much hassle about it. No ghettos, for instance. I am fascinated by the foreign, and I talk to many people in the streets and shops. It's a privilege of age to do so without giving offense. I like or love many people. Yet I regard us humans as a bad lot. Perhaps tribalisms of various kinds form part of the problem. There is a depressing sense of *Der Untergang des Abendlandes* [*The Decline of the West*]. And yet, and yet . . . Here in Europe we are undergoing a unique social experiment, the European Union. Religion, coupled with territorial and dynastic additives, has in the past soaked the soils of Europe with blood from one end to the other; now we sit around a table in Brussels and argue out our differences. Reason has spurred this revolution, not religion.

DR: Dawkins is of course a champion of pure science. But in *HARM*, science does not come off much better than religion, at least in such proponents as Tolsteem and Safelkty.

BA: I admire Richard Dawkins, who was born with many gifts, and have spoken to him about the novel I am currently writing. The humans on Stygia are in part ruined by technology. You can't have better dentistry without dropping an atomic bomb first, you have to go through electronic typewriters to get to the bliss of an iPod, you can't eat strawberries in the winter without overwarming the world . . . Like the incoming tide, science advances on all fronts. Stygian science is mostly forbidden. It is given no chance to develop on the barbaric insect planet.

DR: In many novels with this kind of dual structure, the fantastic world functions as a utopian escape from a less-pleasant reality. But in *HARM*, that is not the case; in fact, the fantastic world recapitulates the "real" world in disturbing ways, not the least of which is the extermination of the indigenous intelligent species of Stygia. I was wondering how much your wartime experiences in Burma contributed to your devastating portrait of a "new" civilization arising on Stygia from the fragments of the old?

BA: Burma illustrates my previous point. On leaving Burma, the British erected a memorial with an epigram carved into the stone. It read:

> *When you go home, think of us and say*
> *For your tomorrow we gave our today.*

I like the sentiments, but who are these "yous" for which we gave our today? The country once known as the Rice Bowl of Asia now lives on handouts, while the lives of ordinary people are prison sentences. As you seem to know, or to guess, Burma somehow always remains in mind, whatever else gets forgotten.

DR: Following is a quote from the last interview I had the pleasure of conducting with you, back in 2000, in connection with *White Mars*:

> Perhaps the further evolution of humankind does require some sort of collaboration; at present almost a quarter of humanity is disenfranchised, starved, exploited. Could we not do better? Why does pity not move us? These are questions worth asking. I have no great faith in utopias ever being established, but questions must be posed now and again. Could we not do better? Is not the West at present in a position to do better?

How do these words resonate for you today? *White Mars*—which, like *HARM*, features an attempt to build a utopia on another world—seems a much more hopeful book than this one. Have you become more pessimistic about humanity's future?

BA: I have become less optimistic about today. Many people have taken refuge in Britain from dirty, dusty villages in the Middle East. They neither know nor understand the West. Consequently, many would destroy it. They have never heard of that ancient piece of sound advice: "When in Rome, do as the Romans do."

DR: I know you've been hard at work on a new novel, *Walcot*. What can you tell us about that?

BA: *Walcot* is the story of a family living throughout the twentieth century. Great world events mingle with small family affairs. It is a narrative very hard to get "right." It took me three long years to compose. I wrote draft after draft, sometimes laughing, often driven to tears. So far, it has brought me not a penny—nor was there a financial reason for writing it. I just wanted to say things that had eluded speech. Of course, it is an English family. What else do I know? You don't happen to know an Anglophile American publisher who might be interested, do you?

DR: I wish I did! It's incomprehensible to me that a writer of your proven gifts and stature could have difficulty placing a novel. Does this discourage you? Do you ever think about retiring? You seem more productive in your eighties than most writers half your age!

BA: No, I do not plan to retire. I enjoy the thought-adventure of writing. On the whole, I find that being eighty is more pleasant than being adolescent. I was encouraged by the award of an O.B.E., which made me think that someone must have been listening. True, a few aches and pains accumulate, but you can edit those out, on the whole. Every day, when awakening, you think what a surprise and joy it is still to be here, some wits remaining, and—with luck—still being published.

We were travelling, four of us, through beautiful unspoilt countryside. We admitted to a guilty pleasure because this halycon wilderness made us think that England must once have looked like this, in the Middle Ages, before clocks chimed or modernity was heard of.

Our vehicle climbed a low hill. As we came down into the vale on the other side, we saw a gaggle of mainly women, standing under a magnificent tree. A black horse was hanging by its neck from a branch. Blowflies buzzed everywhere. A man with a large knife was cutting strips from the horse's body and selling the strips to the women.

This was in Albania, shortly after the dictator, Enver Hoxha, had died.

Maturity: perhaps maturity means finding a way to move with equanimity between the contrapuntal intricacies of joy and anguish, action and thought, fire and calm, love and dismay – all those things which underlie our engagement with experience. Not to be indifferent. Not to be indifferent to the sight we witnessed in Albania: to feel for the poverty to which those women had been reduced, to feel for the savagery of the butcher, perhaps to feel for the remorseless unwinding of history.

Boyhood: that was enlivened and enlightened by reading Editor John Campbell's *Astounding*. I read much else besides, but it was on *Astounding* that my imagination mainly fed. My style came from elsewhere, from Hardy, from Swift, from Dickens, and the poems of Alexander Pope.

I was always glad of the umbrella that the SF field provided. Most of my friends hail from there. Only gradually have I come to believe that many writers were reduced to hacking strips off an old carcass. My claim, my passport, is that I am a Steppenwolf. But then, all true writers are Steppenwolves. They live amid human societies – and some societies are decidedly more desirable than others – but always they have their quarrels, their differences.

HARM's another such one.

BRIAN W. ALDISS served in the Royal Corps of Signals during World War II. When finally demobilised, he went to work in an Oxford bookshop, soon becoming literary editor of *The Oxford Mail* in its pre-tabloid days. He had been writing stories since the age of four and his first professional book, *The Brightfount Diaries*, was published in 1955, the year his first son was born. Since then he has written prolifically, producing novels with some regularity. Best known for his science fiction, he has also produced a string of novels dealing with the issues of ordinary life, many short stories, articles and art works. Three of his works have been filmed: Roger Corman filmed *Frankenstein Unbound*; Stanley Kubrick and Stephen Spielberg between them filmed the short story 'Supertoys Last All Summer Long' (as *A.I.*); while director Keith Fulton filmed *Brothers of the Head* in 2006. Aldiss was awarded an O.B.E. in 2005. Another novel, entitled *Walcot*, the story of an English family living through the twentieth century, will appear in the autumn.